There was silence for such a
if there was a problem with
Finally, Rose asked, "And so what happens if you get
pregnant, and you're too young to actually have a baby?"

Defying all laws of inertia, the acceleration of Kennedy's heart rate crashed to a halt like a car plowing into a brick wall. "What do you mean?"

"Like, what if you're too young but you still get pregnant?"

"How young?" Kennedy spoke both words clearly and slowly, as if rushing might drive the timid voice away for good.

"Like thirteen."

Praise for *Unplanned* by Alana Terry

"Deals with **one of the most difficult situations a pregnancy center could ever face**. The message is **powerful** and the story-telling **compelling**." ~ William Donovan, *Executive Director Anchorage Community Pregnancy Center*

"Alana Terry does an amazing job tackling a very **sensitive subject from the mother's perspective**." ~ Pamela McDonald, *Director Okanogan CareNet Pregnancy Center*

"**Thought-provoking** and intense ... Shows **different sides of the abortion argument**." ~ Sharee Stover, *Wordy Nerdy*

"Alana has a way of sharing the gospel **without being preachy**." ~ Phyllis Sather, *Purposeful Planning*

She wouldn't be victimized again. She had to get away. She wouldn't let him catch up to her. A footstep on the concrete. Not a fabrication. Not this time. It was real. Real as the scientific method. Real as her parents' love for her. Real as death. In the pitch darkness, she rushed ahead, running her fingers along the grimy wall so she would know which way to go as she sprinted down the walkway. What did contracting a few germs compare to getting murdered?

How close was he now? And why couldn't she have remembered her pepper spray? She strained her ears but only heard the slap of her boots on the walkway, the sound of her own panting, the pounding of her heart valves in her pericardial sac. She didn't want to stop, couldn't slow down, but she had to save her strength. She needed energy to fight back when he caught up. She couldn't hear him, but that didn't mean he wasn't coming.

Any second now.

Praise for *Paralyzed* by Alana Terry

"Alana Terry has **done the almost unthinkable**; she has written a story with **raw emotions of real people**, not the usual glossy Christian image." ~ Jasmine Augustine, Tell Tale Book Reviews

"Alana has a way of **using fiction to open difficult issues** and make you think." ~ Phyllis Sather, Author of *Purposeful Planning*

"Once again, Ms. Terry brings a **sensitive but important issue to the forefront** without giving an answer. She **leaves it up to the reader** to think about and decide." ~ Darla Meyer, Book Reviewer

Without warning, the officer punched Reuben in the gut. Reuben doubled over as the cop brought his knee up to his face. Reuben staggered.

"You dirty n—." Without warning, the cop whipped out his pistol and smashed its butt against Reuben's head. He crumpled to the ground, where the officer's boots were ready to meet him with several well-placed kicks.

Throwing all rational thoughts aside, Kennedy jumped on his back. Anything to get him to stop beating Reuben. The officer swore and swatted at her. Kennedy heard herself screaming but had no idea what she was saying. She couldn't see anything else, nor could she understand how it was that when her normal vision returned, she was lying on her back, but the officer and Reuben were nowhere to be seen.

Praise for *Policed* by Alana Terry

"*Policed* could be taken **from the headlines of today's news**." ~ Meagan Myhren-Bennett, *Blooming with Books*

"**A provocative story** with authentic characters." ~ Sheila McIntyre, *Book Reviewer*

"It is important for Christian novelists to address today's issues like police misconduct and racism. Too often writers tiptoe around **serious issues faced by society**." ~ Wesley Harris, *Law Enforcement Veteran*

"Focuses on a prevalent issue in today's society. Alana **pushes the boundaries more than any other Christian writer**." ~ Angie Stormer, *Readaholic Zone*

Wayne Abernathy, the Massachusetts state senator, was towering over a teenage boy who sat crumpled over the Lindgrens' dining room table.

"I don't care what you have to do to fix him," Wayne blasted at Carl.

Kennedy froze. Nobody heard her enter. Carl sat with his back to her, but she could still read the exhaustion in his posture.

Wayne brought his finger inches from the boy's nose. "Do whatever you have to do, Pastor. Either straighten him up, or so help me, he's got to find some other place to live."

Kennedy bit her lip, trying to decide if it would be more awkward to leave, make her presence known, or stay absolutely still.

Wayne's forehead beaded with sweat, and his voice quivered with conviction. "It's impossible for any son of mine to turn out gay."

Praise for *Straightened*
by Alana Terry

"Alana doesn't take a side, but she makes you really think. She **presents both sides of the argument in a very well written way.**" ~ Diane Higgins, *The Book Club Network*

"No matter what conviction you have on the subject, I'm fairly certain **you will find that this novel has a character who accurately represents that viewpoint.**" ~ Justin, Avid Reader

"Alana Terry doesn't beat up her readers, but, rather she gets them to either examine their own beliefs or encourages them to **find out for themselves what they believe and what the Bible says.**" ~ Jasmine Augustine, *Tell Tale Book Reviews*

She shook her head. "I don't know. I can't say. I just know that something is wrong here. It's not safe." She clenched his arm with white knuckles. "Please, I can't ... We have to ..." She bit her lip.

He frowned and let out a heavy sigh. "You're absolutely certain?"

She nodded faintly. "I think so."

"It's probably just nerves. It's been a hard week for all of us." There was a hopefulness in his voice but resignation in his eyes.

She sucked in her breath. "This is different. Please." She drew her son closer to her and lowered her voice. "For the children."

"All right." He unbuckled his seatbelt and signaled one of the flight attendants. "I'm so sorry to cause a problem," he told her when she arrived in the aisle, "but you need to get my family off this plane. Immediately."

Praise for *Turbulence* by Alana Terry

"This book is **hard to put down** and is a **suspenseful roller coaster of twists and turns**." ~ Karen Brooks, *The Book Club Network*

"I've enjoyed all of the Kennedy Stern novels so far, but **this one got to me in a more personal way** than the others have." ~ *Fiction Aficionado*

"I love that the author is **not afraid to deal with tough issues all believers deal with**." ~ Kit Hackett, *YWAM Missionary*

"Blessed are those who are persecuted because of righteousness, for theirs is the kingdom of heaven."

Matthew 5:10

This novel is dedicated to you — all those who have enthusiastically followed Kennedy through her adventures to this point and walked by her side while God has brought her safe thus far.

Note: The views of the characters in this novel do not necessarily reflect the views of the author, nor is their behavior necessarily being condoned.

The characters in this book are fictional. Any resemblance to real persons is coincidental. No part of this book may be reproduced in any form (electronic, audio, print, film, etc.) without the author's written consent.

Captivated
Copyright © 2018 Alana Terry
978-1-941735-52-7
April, 2018

Cover design by Victoria Cooper.

Scriptures quoted from THE HOLY BIBLE, NEW INTERNATIONAL VERSION®, NIV® Copyright © 1973, 1978, 1984, 2011 by Biblica, Inc.® Used by permission. All rights reserved worldwide.

www.alanaterry.com

Captivated

a novel by Alana Terry

ALANA TERRY

PART ONE

CHAPTER 1

"I had a great summer." Ian reached out his hand and caressed Kennedy's cheek with the back of his finger.

She tried to pull her gaze away from him, knowing that what she had to say would come so much more easily if she weren't staring him in the face. If she didn't have to watch his expression change as he realized what she was doing.

She wanted to remember this moment exactly as it was now.

Not like it would be in another minute.

"I'm so glad you agreed to go to Seoul with me," he said. "I'll never forget these past few months."

"Neither will I," Kennedy answered truthfully. She tried to keep her sigh from sounding too melodramatic. After tonight, the memories of their summer together would be bittersweet for both of them.

Maybe it didn't have to happen now. The summer camp for North Korean refugees was over, and this was her last night at her parents' mission home in China. She could call him tomorrow when she landed in Boston, give him the news then. That way she wouldn't have to see his reaction at all.

There was a soft breeze in Yanji, and he wrapped his arm around her as if he were trying to ward off the cold. He didn't deserve to be crushed like this, but after she'd made up her mind, she couldn't change it any more than she could reverse the seasons. Keep the summer from turning into a cool, crisp fall.

"You aren't saying much," Ian observed. "What are you thinking about?"

What was she thinking? How frightened she'd been to spend her summer in Seoul working with people she'd never met. Thinking about what would happen when she hopped on that plane for Logan Airport tomorrow to begin her senior year at Harvard, wondering if deferring her med school admission for a year really was the right choice.

But most of all, she was thinking about Ian. About his shocking red hair that had served to open dozens of conversations with the North Korean refugees they met over the summer in Seoul. The way he'd always been so supportive of her academic goals. The way his skin felt when she ran her palm across his cheek. That exact moment when they'd gone from two acquaintances who occasionally shared breakfast together to a couple.

Most importantly, Kennedy was wondering how he'd react when she broke up with him.

She glanced up into his green eyes. How many late nights had they spent at summer camp, sitting by a bonfire or relaxing in lounge chairs at the conference center on the little island outside of Seoul? How many hours a day had they filled talking about their pasts — about Ian's childhood after his mother died, the eccentric granny who helped raise him and his sister, how he'd thrown off the confines of his religious upbringing in college but was willing to entertain the possibility that his spiritual old granny had been right.

They'd had so many deep discussions about faith, and even though Kennedy had watched Ian soften his views from diehard atheism to curious agnostic, he'd never taken the final step of embracing the truth of Scripture.

She'd been so convinced it would work, no matter how many times in the past her dad had warned her against the dangers of missionary dating. She'd jumped headfirst into a summer fling hoping that by the time she went back to college, God would have changed Ian's mind.

Which he hadn't. No matter how hard or fervently Kennedy wished it. No matter how many times she prayed with her best friend in Alaska. In spite of all of Willow's prayers and hers, Ian wouldn't accept the Jesus he'd grown up worshiping. He didn't tease Kennedy for her faith. In fact, he told her several times how deeply he admired her convictions. Kennedy spent her summer pretending that this budding romance would mean enough to Ian that he'd become a Christian just like her, but now she had to face the truth.

Summer was over. Tomorrow she was heading back to college, and if Ian was really the right man for her, he would have given his life to Christ by now.

She hadn't even told him that she'd emailed the dean to defer her med school admissions. He didn't know that in nine months, Kennedy would return to Seoul to work as an intern for Korea Freedom International, the group that had sponsored the summer camp where they worked.

He didn't know that this time together in the cooling Yanji air would be their very last.

She took a deep breath.

"What is it?" he asked.

He was so observant. Maybe that's why he was such a good photojournalist. Always looking. Perceiving intuitively what language alone could never capture.

She forced herself to meet his gaze, etched each detail of his features into her memory.

"What?" he repeated. Did he guess? Would he have any

idea?

She had to follow through. She couldn't back out now. "I have something we need to talk about. Something important."

CHAPTER 2

"Do you hate me now?" Kennedy's voice was squeaky, but she dared to look up at her boyfriend.

No, make that her ex-boyfriend as of about ten seconds ago.

Ian shook his head. "You know I could never hate you."

She kept waiting for him to say something else. But what?

What was left that hadn't already been said?

"This probably doesn't help," she offered, "but you know it has nothing to do with how much I like you."

Ian sighed. "I know."

They were sitting on a bench, watching the colorful lights in the busyness of Yanji's nightlife.

"Aren't you going to say anything else?"

He shrugged. "Like what? You've made up your mind. I knew from the beginning your faith was important to you. If I were to ask you to change your beliefs, I'd be asking you to fundamentally change who you are, and I don't want to do that. Because I love who you are."

She straightened an invisible wrinkle on her blouse. "Don't talk like that. It just makes it harder."

"You were honest with me. It's only fair for me to be honest with you." He turned to her with a look that was so poignant it felt as if he'd reached through her sternum and was squeezing her heart. "You know I respect your beliefs. I understand that this is the decision you feel is best for you, so I guess that's it."

"Unless ..." Kennedy bit her lip. She hadn't meant to let the word slip.

"Unless what?" He frowned. "Unless I get on my knees and say the sinner's prayer like I did with Grandma Lucy when I was six? Unless I find a pastor in Yanji and get baptized again just like I did when I was twelve?" He shook his head. "I've got my beliefs too. You know that. And one of the things I loved about our time together was that even though Christianity is such an important part of your life, you were okay with all my questions and doubts. Never tried to make me feel bad or as if I'm not as good or as righteous as you."

"You know I don't think about it that way," she began, but Ian cut her off.

"You don't have to explain anything. I get it. I'm sorry

I'm not clapping my hands and jumping up and down because you're doing what you think is right. I realize this is your decision to make, but that doesn't mean it's easy."

Kennedy stared at her lap. "I know. I'm sorry."

"Don't be." He glanced over and offered a brief smile. "I knew what I was getting into when we started dating. Earlier in the summer I called my sister and told her that you'd either be the girl to bring the wayward son home like Grandma Lucy's always praying will happen, or you'd break up with me when you realized it went against your conscience to get involved with someone who didn't see God exactly the same way you do."

Kennedy opened her mouth to object, but Ian put his finger on her lips.

"You don't have to say anything, and you don't have to feel guilty. What I told my sister was that even if things didn't work out between us, if our differences in faith proved to be insurmountable like they have, I would still consider myself a better person for the time we spent together. For the chance to share a little bit of your heart and your life and your love. And when I look at it like that, I don't regret a thing."

A tear slipped down her cheek. He wiped it away with his thumb and kept his hand there, gently cupping her face.

His eyes were full of both joy and sadness. "We had a good summer, didn't we?"

She sniffed and tried to laugh. "Yeah, we did."

"Remember when Jin-Sun put on that wig and did his Sarah Palin impression?"

This time, Kennedy really did laugh. "Or when Mena sprained her ankle during the Gangnam Style dance off?"

His hand still caressed the side of her face. "Remember our first kiss?"

Kennedy tried to look away but couldn't.

"Remember how embarrassed you got when we realized we weren't quite as hidden as we thought we were?"

Kennedy put her hand on top of his, but she wasn't sure if she was holding it even closer against her cheek or trying to push him away.

"I never want to forget," she whispered.

"Me neither." He was leaning toward her now, the same intense gaze that she remembered right before their first kiss.

"One more for the road?" He was asking for her permission.

Maybe it was a dumb idea. Maybe she'd regret it. But she had piled up regrets over the summer like she used to collect antique books.

What could one more hurt?

She blinked back her tears and nodded.

"One more," she answered and anticipated the warmth of his lips.

CHAPTER 3

"You okay, Kensie girl?"

Kennedy glanced up from her half-filled suitcase as her dad stepped into her room. She couldn't quite remember when her parents' house in Yanji had stopped feeling like home. Nice as it was to spend this last week of her summer break with her parents, she was ready to head back to Boston.

"How's the packing going?" her dad asked.

Kennedy grabbed a pile of books and shoved them into her carry-on.

He picked one up. "You've been so busy with Ian all summer, we've hardly talked. I don't even know what you've been reading lately."

Kennedy glanced at the title. "That one's a collection of stories about Christian martyrs. Sandy recommended it."

Her dad flipped through the pages and frowned. "Not quite light reading, is it?"

Kennedy didn't respond.

Her dad sat on the edge of her bed. "How are you really

doing, Princess?"

She shrugged. "I was hoping to be packed by now, but I'll have a little time in the morning before we leave for the airport."

Her dad sighed. "You know that's not what I'm talking about."

What did he expect her to say? That she'd spent every second during the past two hours remembering the exact feel of Ian's lips on hers, knowing that their goodbye kiss would be their last? That for all she told Ian about not regretting how close they'd grown this summer, she realized it was all a lie?

Better to have loved and lost? Not even close.

Her dad reached out to touch her cheek, but Kennedy pulled away. "I'm fine," she snapped then forced a smile to retroactively soften her response. "I'm just a little distracted with packing. That's all."

Her dad stood to leave. "Well, as hard as it was, and as much as your mother and I both liked Ian, I'm proud of you for making the right choice."

The right choice. Her parents must have used that phrase a dozen times since she came home with the news of her breakup, but if Kennedy had really made the right choice, she wouldn't have started dating an unbeliever in the first place.

What was it about that bonfire in Seoul? That

unforgettable moment ...

A summer fling. Kennedy was far from experienced in the dating world, but there was no other name to call it. Still, the phrase certainly didn't do justice to the intensity of her emotions, either before or after she and Ian broke up.

"Got your passport?" her dad asked from the doorway.

"Yeah." She'd made this trip between Yanji and Boston over half a dozen times. She knew what she had to pack. It was just a matter of finding the mental energy to do it.

Her phone beeped. She reached over to look at the text, hating herself for hoping it might be from him.

There's something I want to tell you. Can we meet?

Kennedy knew Ian. Knew he wasn't the type to back her into a corner to get her to change her mind. He understood they were through. His goodbye kiss would have told her that much even if he hadn't said so in words.

She glanced at her clock. Her parents would whine about her going out so late, but they couldn't do much to stop her.

She stared down at her phone, her pulse still slightly elevated at the memory of their parting. She glanced at her suitcase, grabbed a sweater, and typed, *Where do you want to meet?*

CHAPTER 4

Her heart galloped in her chest. Why did Ian want to meet with her? And what should she say when she saw him?

She glanced around at the surroundings. She knew the little café. It catered to English-speaking expats in Yanji, and she and her parents had met Ian here the first day of summer vacation.

Had that really only been just a few months ago?

So much had changed this year, perhaps more than any other she'd spent at Harvard. Her roommate, Willow, had gotten married over Christmas break and was now busy transforming her grandfather's homesteading cabin in Alaska into a foster home. Kennedy had spent the last half of her junior year of college without a roommate. By the time she finished studying for her MCAT in the spring, she had so much free time on her hands she started volunteering twice a week, one afternoon leading the Good News Club at a local elementary school and one afternoon giving English lessons for the Korean-speaking members at St. Margaret's sister church.

She had also spent some of her extra time praying.

Did God really want her to become a doctor? Or was that just a dream she'd latched onto?

Then came summer and the opportunity to work with North Korean refugees in Seoul, seeing Korea Freedom International's ministry firsthand. She'd been honored when the director asked her to come back to serve as an intern after graduation, but now that she'd actually made her medical school deferment official, she stayed awake nearly every night wondering if she'd done the wrong thing.

And of course, there was her relationship with Ian.

Who apparently was just one more thing God was asking her to give up.

She pulled out her phone and glanced at her cell. Her boyfriend was never late.

No, not her boyfriend. Not anymore. How long would it take her to stop using that word?

Then again, *ex* sounded so harsh. Like they both hated each other and had just gone through some sort of nasty breakup. Maybe it would be easier if they had. Easier to break up with someone she despised than someone she still loved.

She sighed. What was taking him so long?

"Kennedy?"

She glanced up as he hurried to her, breathless. "I need to talk to you."

"I assumed that when I got your text." Her joke fell flat, and she offered a small smile in apology.

"Can I sit down?"

What did he expect? That since they weren't officially dating anymore she'd refuse to let him pull up a chair? "Of course you can."

He let out his breath. "This isn't going to work."

She glanced around, hoping for some kind of visual clue that would give a hint as to what he might be talking about. "What isn't?"

"Never seeing you again."

She lowered her gaze. She didn't have the energy for this conversation. Not tonight, when she should already be in bed, resting up for her full day of travel tomorrow.

"Listen," she began, "you know I still really care for you, and this isn't easy for me either ..."

He shook his head to stop her. "You don't get it. I started thinking, and here's what I realized. The thing that makes us so good together is we don't try to change each other. We don't try to turn each other into little clones of ourselves. We can stay up until one or two in the morning talking about abortion or politics or free speech or feminism, and maybe we don't see eye to eye on every single issue, but that's what I love about you. That's what I love about us.

"You never once made me feel bad for not being a Christian. And I guess you were hoping that one day I might become one, but you never made a big deal about it until tonight. Even then, it wasn't like you came to me and said *you've got to convert or we're breaking up*. In fact, I doubt the thought even crossed your mind. You're too respectful for that, so you just called it off without even giving me a chance to think about it.

"Well, I have been thinking about it, and you're right about one thing. I'm not ready to convert. I'm not ready to throw away my textbooks and my scientific proofs and go out on a limb and say *Jesus is the only way to heaven* when that's not what I believe. You and I both know that I could just go through the motions to make you happy, but then our entire relationship would be based on a lie, and one of the greatest strengths I'd say we've got between us is how honest we are.

"So here's what I've decided. I don't want to give up on us. I don't think that's what either of us needs. You spent all of last semester after your roommate got married alone in your dorm room, and I wasn't there to take you out for breakfast or whisk you off campus to go on grand adventures. But I'm wrapping up my work here. I could be back in Cambridge in a week or two, and I don't want to spend all my free time in my studio staring at the walls any more than you want to be stuck in your dorm.

"Maybe we don't have the same religious beliefs yet, but our conversations have given me a lot to think about. Even that science book your dad loaned me about evolution and creation, it gave me a ton to digest and sit on. And what I really need at this point in my spiritual journey is someone who I can talk to about all these ideas, someone who isn't trying to change my mind and isn't afraid of my questions. I'm not even asking you to be my girlfriend again if the whole faith thing truly is a deal-breaker for you, but I'm not about to just let our friendship go extinct. Get what I'm saying?"

Kennedy blinked. Did she?

"What exactly are you proposing?" she asked.

"I wish I knew. Just something more than goodbye." For the first time, he cracked a small smile.

It would have felt so natural for her to reach out and take his hand, but she tightened her fist and kept it in her lap.

"Friends?" he asked.

A dozen different warnings whizzed through her head, telling her that she needed to think and pray through any major decision before she made up her mind. She bit her lip before she could say anything.

"You need more time, don't you?"

She nodded, thankful he could read her hesitation. Had she hurt his feelings?

He stood up. "Well, can I at least walk you back to your parents'?"

She glanced up at him and felt her face flush when she remembered the passion of his kiss just a few hours earlier. "Yeah," she answered. "That'd be nice."

CHAPTER 5

"It's a quiet night, isn't it?" Ian asked.

She nodded, wondering if he meant to take the roundabout way back to her parents' neighborhood or if he simply wasn't as familiar with Yanji as she was. She'd spent half her childhood and most of her teen years here. At certain points in her life, it had felt more like home than anywhere in the States.

In other ways, she still felt like a stranger here.

Their conversation had been strained during their entire walk. Maybe it was just because she was so tired. What had they spent all summer yakking about?

"How's the documentary coming?" she finally asked.

Ian could always talk about his work.

He sighed. "I wish I could head back into North Korea to shoot a little more footage." Several years earlier, he'd been invited to Pyongyang on a tourist visa but had gotten in trouble with government officials when they caught him trying to sneak unauthorized photographs out of the country.

"That boy you met made a big impact on you, didn't he?" Kennedy asked. Over the summer in Seoul, Ian had told her about one of the homeless children he'd photographed foraging for roots north of Pyongyang. Something in the boy's expression had branded itself onto Ian's soul. Every time he talked about the little flower swallow, Kennedy got the sense that she was getting to know a real child, not some nameless statistic.

"Have you tried getting another visa?" she asked.

He shook his head. "No. They know I'm a journalist now. They've probably seen some of my interviews with defectors in China. I'd be in huge trouble if I tried getting back in."

"Just promise me you won't try to sneak over the border then." She was trying to make a joke, but his silence was far from reassuring. She paused by an alleyway. "Wait a minute. You aren't seriously thinking about that, are you?"

He shook his head. "No. No, I wouldn't do anything that stupid."

"Good." She'd been preparing to tell him about all the Americans who'd been imprisoned in North Korea over the past five years — two journalists who tried to sneak across the border from China, a pastor who was on his way to make a prayer vigil to Pyongyang, even that poor college student who'd only wanted to see part of the world hardly anyone else in America had.

They resumed their walk. In ten minutes, they'd be back in front of her parents' home, and it would be time for one last goodbye. It was too bad they'd broken up. Even though it was August, the night air was chilly, and she could have used his warm arm tight around her.

Ian didn't talk. Was he thinking about that street kid? Tomorrow, she'd probably feel embarrassed at how she'd made him promise not to try to return to North Korea, but tonight, she was just glad he'd given her his word.

They weren't dating anymore, but that wouldn't stop her from worrying about him.

Maybe she'd always worry about him.

Her steps fell heavy on the sidewalk. Would the night ever end?

Her parents' house loomed into view. As a teenager, she hadn't thought twice about the mansion her parents owned in this upscale neighborhood for foreigners, but now that she'd seen how many people lived in poverty or suffered under the weight of injustice, she was ashamed at the grotesque opulence. At least her mom and dad put their home to good use. They almost always had a small live-in staff to help manage the gardening, the cooking, the cleaning, everything. Most of these were North Korean refugees, which is how Kennedy learned Korean growing up.

The Chinese police had gotten stricter about anyone, foreigner or not, aiding defectors, so her parents had to be extra careful with whom they hired, but thankfully God protected them for over ten years and allowed them to continue serving here in Yanji.

"Wait a minute." Ian grabbed her by the arm, but there was nothing inviting or romantic about his touch.

"What is that?" Kennedy had been so absorbed in her thoughts she didn't notice the police cars.

A flashlight shined toward them, and she was momentarily blinded.

"Get behind me," Ian ordered.

A policeman shouted something at them.

"Kennedy, run." Ian shoved her away, and she nearly tripped. A whistle blew in her ears, loud and shrill.

She only made it a few feet before someone tackled her from behind.

A blow to her head.

She couldn't see or hear anything.

CHAPTER 6

Someone was holding her, keeping her steady. Protecting her from the cold.

She tried to open her eyes, but her head hurt too much to see anything. It was still dark. That much she knew.

Bumpy. Were they in a car? What was that on her wrists?

"Kennedy?" a kind voice whispered. "Are you awake?"

She tried to nod her head, but it rolled to the side again. Sleep.

All she wanted to do was sleep, and in the morning, she'd wake up at the summer camp in Seoul and tell her boyfriend about the bizarre dream she'd had.

***

"Give me your name." The officer shouted at her in Korean but wore the uniform of the Chinese police.

"Give me your name," he repeated in a gruff voice.

"Kennedy." She licked her lips. How long had she gone without any water? "Kennedy Stern. I'm an American. I want to speak with someone from the US embassy." How many times had her dad made her recite those words since they moved to China? She could say them in three different languages but never thought she'd have to use them in a crisis situation.

She didn't like how many times in the past several years her dad's apparently outlandish fears and paranoid training had proven useful.

"The consulate," she demanded in English, in case he hadn't understood her Korean.

He shook his head. "First you will answer a few questions for us. Then we'll see about contacting the embassy." He picked up a glass of water that was just out of her reach. Kennedy had been handcuffed to a desk all night. Maybe longer. She'd dozed off several times before finally waking up for good, sore and disoriented.

"The American you're with. The one with the red hair. What's his name?"

Kennedy had lost track of how many dozens of times he'd asked her this or similar questions. She refused to tell him anything, just like her dad taught her, reminding the guard that she was an American and had every right to speak to her consul.

He shook his head. "You must be thirsty, no?" He held up his glass and made a noisy show of finishing the water off. Kennedy's throat nearly seized shut, and she licked her dry lips once more.

"What's the name of that redheaded American?"

She stared at the guard's polished boots, trying to figure out what it meant that he was far more concerned about Ian than he was about her or her parents.

"Let's make it simple," he said. "You tell me his name, I give you a drink. Who is he?"

Kennedy tried not to glance at Ian's picture on the desk.

"What if I told you that I already know who he is? Does that make it easier? Former film and journalism student from Harvard University. Grew up in the state of Washington. See? You won't be telling me anything that I don't already know." He cleared his throat and poured the water into the empty cup, holding it up to her. "What's his name?"

She tried her best to take in a deep breath. "Ian McAllister," she answered. "His name is Ian McAllister."

CHAPTER 7

She shouldn't have read all those testimonies about Christian martyrs. For however long it'd been, for however long she'd been stuck here alone in this dark cell, her brain kept bringing to mind tales of torture and gruesome deaths from the time of the Roman Coliseum to the present day.

These stories of triumph in the face of suffering and persecution were encouraging and inspirational, but Kennedy didn't need inspiration at the moment. She needed the consulate.

She had answered several of the guard's questions about Ian, nothing that couldn't be found through a quick Google search. In so doing, she earned herself a full cup of water, a trip to the bathroom, and some hard, tasteless bread.

When the man started to ask her about the documentary Ian was producing about North Korean defectors, she reminded him again that he was obligated to get in touch with the American Embassy on her behalf.

That had been hours ago, although without windows,

there was no objective way to mark the passing of time. She tried to doze. Her head still ached from when she'd been attacked.

And now she was sitting here in darkness, with no consul to speak to, no parents frantically trying to get hold of her on her cell, and no Ian.

Where was he? When she'd seen the police in front of her house, she'd been certain they were there to question her parents about their ministry to illegal North Korean refugees. But her interrogator hadn't asked a single question about them.

What was happening to Ian? She had vague memories of him holding her while they transported her here, wherever here was, but she'd been so out of it that could easily be some sort of dream or delusion. Was he safe?

Was she?

What a stupid question. Of course she was. She was an American citizen, and so was he. Maybe that didn't mean much in a country like North Korea, but here in China missionaries might get questioned. They might get pressed for bribes. In some scenarios, they might even get deported, but that was the worst thing that was allowed to happen to them.

And seeing as how Kennedy was scheduled to fly to Boston tomorrow to start her senior year, deportation was a perfectly acceptable punishment.

If only she could ensure Ian was safe. In the darkness, she ran through the script of her interrogation. Had she incriminated him somehow? Had she given any sort of information that might get him in more trouble than he already was? Ian was an American too, a world traveler with far more experience than she had with visas and diplomacy.

She'd be fine. Give the Chinese police a little bit longer to sort out their paperwork, and any minute someone from the embassy would come in, sign whatever forms were necessary, and escort Kennedy out of here.

Ian too.

She was no longer handcuffed, and she ran her fingers across the cinderblocks of her cell, wondering how soundproof they might be. If she called out to him, would he hear her?

And even if he could, what was there to say?

She leaned with her back against the cold wall, hugged her knees, and refused to give way to the tears that threatened to fall. There was no reason to cry, not when her American passport meant that the consul would come and walk her out of this cell if she could just hold on to hope a little bit longer.

Freedom was coming.

Any minute now…

CHAPTER 8

It was simple kindnesses — like being able to use a real restroom instead of squatting over the pail in the corner of her cell — that convinced Kennedy everything would be fine.

A full day must have passed so far. Maybe more. At one point, she managed to sleep curled up on the floor of her dank cell. She woke up with a sore throat and stiff joints, but she encouraged herself with the thought that today she would be set free.

There was no way the Chinese were brazen enough to hold her here another twenty-four hours.

Hak-Kun, the young guard she'd been assigned after her interrogator was finished with her, asked all sorts of questions about her time on the East Coast. Apparently, he was obsessed with American baseball. It was hard to tell what made him more disappointed, that she'd never gone to a Red Sox game or that she couldn't answer questions about World Series played years before her birth.

Yet another sign that her freedom was imminent. Hak-Kun was as bored as she was, just counting down the minutes until this business got sorted out and they let her free. She didn't have any more information the police needed, except that which might satisfy her guard's curiosity. What were hotdogs made out of? Did every American family really own two cars? Wasn't she scared to go into malls or movie theatres with all those shooters running free with their dozens of guns and slings of ammunition?

He was also interested in improving his English and often asked Kennedy to explain certain idioms. Why would anyone say it was raining cats and dogs instead of fish and sharks? Why do Americans say *hit the sack* instead of *hit the mattress* or *hit the pillow?*

It was almost as if she were back at St. Margaret's Korean-speaking sister church, helping others improve their English conversational skills. Since Kennedy had no idea what time it really was, she decided that the food Hak-Kun most recently brought her was dinner. It was certainly the biggest meal she'd eaten so far, and she was thankful for a bowl of soup, whose broth was perfect for softening her hard-as-cinder-bricks piece of bread.

Hak-Kun sat across from her and watched her eat. If she

hadn't been so hungry, she might have spent more energy wondering if it was rude not to share.

"So, your red-haired friend," Hak-Kun began as Kennedy swallowed down a bite of broth-soaked roll. "How long do you think he's been a spy?"

She was too absorbed with her food to let out a giggle.

Ian? A spy? "I think you're talking about the wrong guy."

Hak-Kun shook his head. "No, we have a record on him. That friend of yours is real trouble. Which makes my superiors curious to know how close the two of you are." He leaned forward and raised his eyebrows.

She'd heard all the time about good cop/bad cop routines, but she never thought one individual might try to play both roles in the same day. Wasn't this the same guard who only an hour or two earlier had asked her the difference between French fries and hash browns? What happened to all his English questions or useless baseball trivia?

"Ian's not a spy." She wasn't sure why she was wasting her words. Did she think that simply telling Hak-Kun the truth enough times would make him believe it?

"Then what's he doing making all these videos?"

"He just wants to show people how hard it is for North

Koreans living in China. That's all."

Hak-Kun scoffed. "It's hard because they're not supposed to be here in the first place. You understand. You Americans hate your illegal immigrants too."

Kennedy didn't feel qualified to dive into a political debate with anybody, American or not. "I don't know about Ian's documentary, but I do know that you have absolutely nothing to worry about. He's a journalist. Not a spy."

Hak-Kun drummed his fingers on the tabletop. "Did you say he's making a documentary?"

Did she? Wasn't that one of the things he had already known about Ian anyway? Why couldn't she remember?

She took another bite of her bread. "Did you get in touch with the embassy yet?" she demanded.

He nodded. Was that a grin on his face? "Yes. They're eager to talk to you, as I'm sure you can imagine."

She had no idea what he meant by that last part, but at least she'd be leaving here. And none too soon. How had the Chinese managed to keep her locked up like this without a major international catastrophe breaking out?

Or maybe it had. Would she be met by dozens of press members when she stepped into the blinding light of day? Maybe she should have a few words prepared. She'd have to ask the consul about that.

"I've cooperated," she reminded Hak-Kun. "You can't keep me here any longer."

This time the grin on his face was unmistakable. "Oh, don't worry. Let's see. How do you Americans put it? *I wouldn't dream of it.*"

CHAPTER 9

"Hak-Kun?" Kennedy called into the darkness. Her ears were still ringing with the sound of her own scream that had woken her up when something scurried across her leg. "Hak-Kun?"

Was it night now? How could he have left her in here? Wasn't she supposed to meet with someone from the Embassy?

Maybe it was just all the time alone without any windows or outside light. Maybe she'd really only been here a few hours total. She tried to count the meals she'd eaten but couldn't remember.

"Hak-Kun?" she called again, straining her eyes to try to detect the rodent that had woken her up.

Tears leaked down her cheeks. This wasn't fair. She'd kept her composure, promised herself that the embassy would get her out of this cell. How many hours, how many days had she been telling herself the exact same thing?

But no consul.

"Hak-Kun?" Her cry echoed off the cinder blocks surrounding her, holding her captive? "Hak-Kun? Anybody?"

Her voice died down along with any hope of rescue. What was the point? She'd been lying to herself for as many hours or days as she'd been trapped down here. Help wasn't coming. These people wanted to know something about Ian, and they weren't going to release her until they got it.

They probably hadn't even contacted the embassy. No, there wasn't even a probably about it. If the embassy knew she was here, they would force the Chinese to free her. Which meant they didn't know where she was, which meant her parents were frantic with worry. She was so nauseated she felt like she was about to throw up whatever contents were left in her stomach from dinner.

"Hak-Kun." She whispered her guard's name. He wasn't here. He'd deserted her. She was alone.

She thought back to that book of martyrs, how glorious their suffering had sounded. Many of them sang hymns in jail or shared the gospel with their captors. All Kennedy had told Hak-Kun was that *Jingle Bells* was a more popular Christmas song than Mariah Carey's *All I Want for Christmas is You*.

And there was certainly nothing glorious about the darkness, the fear, or the hunger.

She screamed again when some creature ran over her shin. How big was that thing?

Her scream turned to sobs. She didn't even try to keep her volume down anymore. What did it matter? She was the only one here.

"Kennedy?"

She sniffed in the darkness, trying to calm down her breathing so she could hear more clearly.

"Kennedy? Is that you? It's me. It's Ian."

The Chinese prison that held her captive was certainly an inappropriate place for laughter, but she let out a chuckle that mingled with her tears. "Ian?" she choked on his name, uncertain if she was laughing or crying.

"Can you hear me? Where are you?" he asked.

"Over here." She waved her hand as if that would do any good in this darkness.

"Are you all right?" he asked. "How long have you been here?"

"I don't know. Two days? I've lost track. Have you been here this whole time?"

"No, they just transferred me here. I was …" His voice trailed off, and then he started again. "I was somewhere else. Thank God you're all right. I've been so worried about you."

"What's going on? What are we doing here?"

"Did they question you?" he asked at the same time. "What did you say?"

She didn't want to talk about her interrogation sessions. She wanted Ian to say something to help make sense of this chaos.

"Nothing. I hardly mentioned anything." Her voice was hoarse from speaking so loudly. Screaming at a rat and then crying over her misfortunes certainly hadn't helped. "Do my parents know where we are?"

"I don't have any more information than you do," he admitted. Not at all what Kennedy had been hoping to hear. "But we're going to be all right."

"What makes you so sure?" She hadn't meant to sound testy, but that was a bold promise coming from someone trapped with her in a Chinese jail cell.

"Because we're together. Trust me. It's all going to turn out just fine."

CHAPTER 10

Kennedy had been right. It was nighttime when she and Ian found each other. By morning, when Hak-Kun turned on the lights, she strained her neck as far as she could, pressing her face against her bars, but she still couldn't make out any other cells. She knew from the sound of his voice last night that Ian was somewhere to her left, at least some distance apart judging by how loudly they had to speak.

She hadn't heard from him since the lights turned on. They'd already decided it wouldn't be safe to communicate if anyone was around.

And so she waited. Thinking about Ian, about the summer they spent together.

Seoul was a considerably bigger city than Yanji, but ironically it felt less congested. She'd spent her first weeks getting to know the people in the Korea Freedom International home office. Mena, the director, was a young newlywed working with her husband, a defector from North Korea. Jin-Sun had spent some time in a North Korean jail before his escape and was missing a few fingers, but he never explained what happened.

While Ian spent his days interviewing the workers at the nonprofit and editing his documents, Kennedy volunteered her services in a number of different ways. Proof-reading emails, setting up an English-speaking social media account, and double-checking some English translations of Korea Freedom's flyers and brochures.

Then they all traveled to a small island just outside of Seoul, with locusts so loud she'd get a headache any time she went out before sunset. Thankfully, the camp was held at a retreat center, with most of the daily activities taking place inside the air-conditioned reception rooms.

But the nights were spent outdoors, with bonfires, laughter, music, and games.

And, of course, Ian.

It was at a bonfire the second week when he'd leaned over and kissed her. She hadn't been ready for it, was terrified that her breath must stink like the fish stew she'd eaten for dinner, but he didn't seem to mind, and she quickly forgot her concerns.

At another bonfire, they stayed up until two in the morning talking about creation science, followed by a lively debate about whether or not Jesus was the only way to heaven. The next night they discussed Washington's response to illegal immigration until one, right after they finished arguing about American education reforms.

But they didn't just talk about religion and politics.

One morning, Ian woke her up early so they could watch the sun rise before the heat and bugs became unbearable, and they spent their time cuddling together and talking about their favorite Charles Dickens novels. Ian told her about his travels. His film work had taken him to a dozen different countries in Asia, and he'd studied abroad in both Greece and Iceland during his time as an undergrad.

He had a little old granny in Washington State he spoke of adoringly, even though he freely admitted she was a religious fanatic, a right-wing Christian fundamentalist who saw it as her life's duty to see every one of her dozens or hundreds of grandchildren and great-grandchildren living moral Christian lives. It seemed there wasn't anything Kennedy and Ian hadn't talked about over the summer.

Except, of course, what might happen if they got in trouble with the Chinese police who refused to grant them access to the American embassy. But she was glad they were together, glad she didn't have to worry about where he was or how badly he was being treated.

Now she'd just have to wait. At some point after dinner, Hak-Kun would turn off the lights before heading home, and they'd be free to talk again.

Nighttime couldn't come quickly enough.

CHAPTER 11

"Come on. Get up."

Kennedy didn't recognize the voice. Where was Hak-Kun? What time was it?

She blinked her eyes open. How long had she been asleep? She'd been talking with Ian after the lights went off. He was telling her about how his grandma had suffered two separate heart attacks, how he was worried that if she found out he was imprisoned she wouldn't be able to handle the shock.

Had Kennedy fallen asleep in the middle of their conversation?

The overhead lights blinded her, and she tried to shield her face when someone entered the cell. Rough hands yanked her to her feet.

"Let's go. Get moving."

She was even thirstier than normal and could barely ask, "Where are we going?"

"Come on."

What about Ian? Was he coming too?

She called his name. No answer. It wasn't until then that her heart started thudding loud enough to hear.

"Where are we going?" she asked again. "Where's Ian?" She dug her heels into the ground, but her impractical fashion boots just slipped right over the concrete floor as the guard dragged her toward a flight of stairs.

"You can't do this." She forced as much confidence as she could into her tone, just like her father had taught her. "I demand to speak with the US consulate. You have no right to take me anywhere."

The man scoffed. "You want to speak with the consulate? Fine. That's where we're going. Hurry up. His Excellency's waiting."

The chuckle he let out chilled the blood in her veins. Her legs nearly collapsed beneath her. The man swore, and all Kennedy could do was manage a faint, whispered prayer.

"Dear Jesus, please get me out of here."

CHAPTER 12

"So that's it? I'm free to go?" Kennedy stared at the round-faced consul who had secured her rescue.

"Yup. Unless you'd care for more coffee or tea before we get you to your parents."

She shook her head, hardly able to believe she was free or that her entire captivity had only lasted three days.

She stood up, grasping her chair for support. She'd eaten a hearty egg and pancake breakfast with the man from the embassy but still felt somewhat nauseated. "And you'll let me know as soon as you hear anything about Ian?"

He nodded. "Unfortunately, as I already explained, now that the Chinese have involved the DPRK government, it's going to be a lot trickier to handle." They'd gone over this countless times already, but Kennedy still didn't understand. How could an American in China get in trouble with the North Korean government for some photos he'd taken years earlier? The consul was sympathetic, but since the US had no diplomatic relationship with North Korea, he told her all she could do now was wait.

"Be thankful you're free," he added, "and trust the official processes to work themselves out as far as your friend is concerned." He hadn't been able to look her in the eye with that last bit.

Well, there was no use pitching a fit here. Her parents were just outside. She couldn't talk to them until getting this last debriefing out of the way, but after a few apologies for how long it had taken them to locate and free her in the first place, coupled with a few more boilerplate assurances that Ian's safety was their top concern, she was led into a small sitting room where her parents were waiting.

Her mom immediately started to cry. After hugging Kennedy, she ran her hands over every part of her body, checking for injuries and asking dozens of questions. "Did they hurt you? Is anything broken? Have you eaten? Why do you look so skinny? Did you get any sleep at all?"

Her father was mostly silent, his drooping eyelids as certain a tell-tale sign of his sleepless nights as the black smudges under his eyes. He hugged her as soon as her mom let go but didn't say anything other than, "I heard about Ian. I'm sorry."

What had he heard? The consul wasn't exactly a reservoir of information. All he'd told Kennedy was that

Ian had been on some sort of North Korean watch list because of his photographs a few years earlier, and it was possible that the Chinese were planning to hand him over to Pyongyang. Even though they'd managed to get Kennedy out, thanks in large part to her father's relentless lobbying on her behalf, the US Embassy hadn't even received official admission from the Chinese that they were holding Ian at all.

She clung to her parents, let her mother fawn over her, and thanked God that she was finally safe. Still, she knew that until she saw Ian standing in front of her in the flesh, the nightmare was far from over.

PART TWO

CHAPTER 13

Two and a half weeks later

Kennedy pulled her phone out of her backpack. Any time it rang, her heart would start pounding in hopes that it would finally be someone who could give her an update on Ian.

"Hello?"

"Hi, sweetie. It's Mom. Did I interrupt something? Are you in the middle of a lecture?"

Kennedy let out her breath. She had been so excited and nervous when the phone rang, she'd answered it before even checking the caller ID.

"No, I'm finished with my classes for the day." She was two weeks into her senior year at Harvard and more behind than she'd been in her entire academic career. The campus counselor she'd been seeing for years thought Kennedy had unresolved trauma from her three-day vacation in a Chinese jail, but she hardly thought about that anymore. All of her mental energy was tied up worrying about Ian. If she'd known that their conversation in the dark would be the last she might ever hear from him, she would have made it a point to stay awake the entire night. Maybe she would have heard something. Some sort of clue regarding his current whereabouts.

"Well," her mom continued, "if you don't have anywhere else to be, I'm going to do a little furniture shopping and wondered if you wanted to tag along."

Kennedy glanced at the time. Her parents had returned to the States the week after she did, having been warned by the consul that now might not be the best time for them to continue their clandestine mission work in Yanji. Her dad was still operating on China time, spending every evening and night on the phone with the manager of his printing business, which meant her mom was left to herself to set up and furnish the little Medford townhouse they were renting.

Kennedy glanced out the window at the students scurrying to and from their afternoon classes. She longed for the days when all she had to get stressed out over were lab reports or her upcoming science tests. "I'm sorry," she answered. "I've got a paper to write for my Dickens class, and I'm still fighting that sore throat. Could we spend some time together tomorrow instead?"

Her mom's voice was full of forced cheer. "That's fine. Maybe I'll call Sandy and see if she's busy. Seems like ever since we got back to town, she and I have only seen each other in passing. You drink lots of tea and get some extra sleep and take good care of yourself. You hear that?"

Kennedy wasn't sure how she felt about having her parents live a twenty-minute drive away instead of a twenty-hour plane flight. It definitely had its advantages, but the new arrangement would take some time to adjust to.

"Oh, before I go," her mom added, "I got another phone call from Ian's grandma. She's a fine Christian woman, you know, and we even prayed together over the phone. Grandma Lucy thinks Ian is going to be just fine, and she's praying for you too. We all are, but I'm sure you know that by now."

Kennedy was ready for the phone call to end. She mumbled her thanks, said goodbye, and stared at the books and folders on her desk. When had she gotten so disorganized? Maybe it was nothing more than a bad case of senioritis. After all, she'd aced her MCAT entrance exams last spring and had already deferred her med school acceptance. She'd planned to spend that year after graduation in Seoul working with Korea Freedom International, but she wasn't even going to think about that right now, not when she could only guess where Ian was.

The Chinese government denied ever holding him in the first place. Kennedy's detainment by contrast had made a very tiny ripple in certain Christian publications as an example of American underground missionaries suffering persecution, but since she'd only been held for a few days and had no real injuries to show for it, and since her parents still needed to downplay their involvement in missions, the story never took off. Which was fine with her. She'd spent enough of her college career in the public eye.

She sank her elbows on her desk and cradled her head in her hands. It was days like this that she missed Willow the most. Why did Alaska have to be so far away?

She never would get her paper written if she kept procrastinating like this, but her mind was too heavy with worry to think through anything clearly. She went to the Korea Freedom International webpage, a deep ache in her soul as she scrolled through pictures of the staff she'd worked with last summer. Why was she torturing herself like this? What did she think it would accomplish? If she wasn't going to write her paper, she should be doing something productive. Petitioning the US government — for the twentieth or thirtieth time — to look more closely into Ian's case. To respond to one of his grandmother's plentiful emails and voice messages. Kennedy had met Grandma Lucy on an airplane, but it wasn't until Ian showed her a picture on his phone she realized the tiny old spitfire of a Christian was related to her boyfriend.

Or ex-boyfriend.

And did it really matter what she called him if he was being held in some jail cell until he died?

She chided herself for her pessimism and rummaged through the folders on her desk until she found the lecture notes from her Dickens class. She had been staring at the instructions for her paper for at least ten minutes when her phone rang again. This time she remembered to check the caller ID.

"Hey, Willow."

After her wedding, Willow and Kennedy had talked on the phone nearly every day, but they'd both had such busy summers that sometimes weeks would go by when all they could do was text.

"Have you seen what's on the news?"

Kennedy's stomach felt as if it were in free fall. She clicked off her screensaver and jumped onto Channel 2's website.

"I didn't know if you'd heard yet," Willow was saying, "but I thought maybe you could use someone to talk to or pray with. We've got a little extra money set aside from last summer's haying, and I could fly out to be with you if you wanted. Kennedy?"

Kennedy had stopped listening and was staring at the screen.

Boston-based journalist imprisoned in North Korea.

CHAPTER 14

"It's going to be all right, honey," her mom said as she stroked Kennedy's hair. "You just wait and see."

Kennedy buried her face in her parents' pillows. Did her mom seriously think that platitudes would help?

Her dad stood in the doorway of the bedroom and cleared his throat. "Sometimes news reports are wrong, Princess," he began. "One could always hope ..."

Sandy, a longtime friend of the family and Kennedy's pastor's wife, clucked her tongue. "Now, you listen to me, pumpkin. What's happening to Ian, if these reports are true, is a real tragedy, and I'm not going to pretend to have the words to say to make you feel better about any of it. None of it's right, nothing at all, but somehow, in the midst of all this confusion and turmoil and sadness, we know that there is a God who loves Ian more than any of us ever could, and he doesn't sleep or faint or grow weary. So you cry all the tears you want. You tell God just how you're feeling, and don't sugarcoat it or pretend or put on your best face or none of that nonsense now. You just remember that when all is said and done, when those tears run dry, that God loves this young man more than you or I could even imagine." She leaned over the bed and rubbed Kennedy's back, the gentle, soothing touch, producing a fresh round of heaving sobs.

"Do you think we should call the doctor?" Kennedy heard her mom ask.

"You just leave her be," Sandy answered, "because it's perfectly natural, this kind of reaction. Sometimes I think that if we really understood how much terrible suffering is going on right in our own backyards, none of us would be able to get out of bed at all."

Her mom started to talk, but Sandy gave a loud shush. "Now, I've got to pick up Woong from his science co-op, but Kennedy knows she can call me any time, night or day. I've got a big pot of chili heating up at home in the crockpot. Should I bring you some a little later this evening?"

Kennedy didn't pay attention to the rest of the conversation. She didn't know if her body was in shock or if it had physically revolted against what she read about in that news article. While her mom walked Sandy out, Kennedy's dad sat beside her on the bed.

"How you holding up, Princess?"

She didn't bother to answer.

"I just checked Channel 2," he said. "No updates yet."

It figured.

"Do you think he's really there?" Her dad was asking her? How should she have any idea? All she knew was the news report was full of lies. They said that Ian had been caught sneaking into North Korea. Kennedy hadn't even started to cry until she read the comments at the bottom of the article.

What's he expect if he goes spying around in a commie country like that?

North Korea's crazy. Why would anybody want to go there in the first place?

And that's why smart people don't try running across borders. If you ask me, the reporter got what's coming to him. Let's just hope they don't send him home in a coma like they did that college kid.

For the past two weeks she'd been telling herself and God that it would be so much easier if she just knew where Ian was. Now she realized having at least some hope was better than this. She didn't need a Google search to find all the stories about how North Korea treated its prisoners. She'd met enough defectors and heard their accounts firsthand.

Still, something had always made it feel foreign. Removed. These things happened to people inside the Hermit Kingdom. Not to Americans.

Not to Ian.

Kennedy's mom came back in, looking tired and somewhat sheepish. "Sweetheart, your phone was ringing." She held out Kennedy's cell. "It's Ian's grandma. Do you feel like talking?"

No, she didn't, but her mom thrust her phone into Kennedy's hand without waiting for an answer.

Kennedy didn't have any choice. "Hi, Grandma Lucy."

"Oh, thank the good Lord I got hold of you. You've heard the news by now, I'm sure." Grandma Lucy's voice was full of cracks and warbles but also a spiritual intensity that could put even the most ardent of believers to shame.

"Yeah, I heard." She sat up in bed and motioned for her parents to leave. "How are you? Does the rest of the family know?"

"We've been calling around since we got the news. A nice young man from the embassy got in touch with us earlier this afternoon, so we heard just a little bit before the press. The whole time I've been praying for my grandson, but the Holy Spirit's been impressing on me to be praying just as hard for you too. How are you? I was so happy when your mom picked up. I didn't like the thought of you being in that dorm room all sad and scared and by yourself."

"I'm all right. Both my parents are here, and my pastor's wife just left."

"Well, good. I can't tell you how much it means to me knowing people are praying for my Ian. I told the Lord just a few minutes ago, I said, *God, thank you that the truth has finally come to light,* because it's the truth that sets us free. You know that, don't you?"

"Yeah. I know." As tired and mentally exhausted as she was, Kennedy still realized that this was a completely backwards conversation. She should be the one offering Ian's grandma comfort. Not the other way around.

"I've been praying for that boy his whole life," Grandma Lucy went on, "and somewhere in my spirit, I said to myself, *Lucy Jean, do you really think you should be praying so hard? Because you know he's the kind of boy that's going to need his world shaken up before he finally gets on his knees and repents of his sins.*"

Kennedy didn't reply. Out of everyone in the entire world, it was possible that she and Grandma Lucy wanted Ian to come to Christ more than anyone else, but that still didn't mean Kennedy would wish any catastrophe like this on him.

"Well, it sounds like you're doing okay," Kennedy said, trying to find the most polite way to move the conversation toward goodbye. "It was nice of you to call."

"Oh, I'm not finished, you know. I have a Bible verse I wanted to pass along. I came across it this morning in my quiet time. There I was, sitting in my prayer chair, just rocking away and about to doze off for my mid-morning nap, when all of a sudden, the Holy Spirit just took me by the shoulders and said, *The truth will set you free.* I'm still praying, asking God for more wisdom to know exactly what he was trying to reveal to me, but I know it has something to do with Ian and the way that boy was blinded by so many lies. He knew the truth once. Back when he was a little boy, he loved Jesus with his whole heart, with that innocent and simple faith of a child. But something happened when he went off to college, and I've been praying ever since that God would take hold of him once more and show him it's only in Jesus the real truth can be found. So I wanted to call and share with you what God had told me earlier, and now I figure since we're on the phone, we may as well pray together. I can guarantee you the devil's going to be doing everything in his power to keep Ian from ever finding the truth. And how could he be free then?"

Without waiting, Grandma Lucy began to pray. Kennedy listened, feeling more like a voyeur than a participant. Even after Grandma Lucy said goodbye, Kennedy mulled over what the old woman had said.

The truth will set you free.

Maybe there was something to her words. At least now that she knew where Ian was, she could pray for him more specifically. That should count for something, right?

She thought back to her time on the phone with Grandma Lucy and decided that if a little old lady who'd already survived two massive heart attacks could devote so much power and energy into her prayers, Kennedy may as well try to do the same.

CHAPTER 15

Three months later

"Dude." Willow's voice from thousands of miles away in Alaska still sounded just as if she was standing behind Kennedy, staring over her shoulder. "What are you going to do?"

Kennedy studied the notebook in her hand, surprised that it looked so normal. For what it contained, she would have expected something entirely different. Something of this magnitude shouldn't feel like plain paper, should it?

"And that's all she said?" Willow asked. "She just said you should read it and left it at that?"

Kennedy didn't have time for this. Her first final was in ten days. She still hadn't completed her *Hard Times* paper, which had been due before Thanksgiving. It was the first time she ever needed to ask a professor for an extension.

In some ways, it was miraculous she was still in college

and hadn't failed every single one of her classes. Some of her motivation came from a few not-so-peppy pep talks with Professor Adell, her former chemistry professor and academic advisor, who made it very clear that if Kennedy couldn't manage to work her way through what should theoretically be an easy sixteen-credits semester, she had no business presuming to belong at Harvard.

And some of her motivation came from the fact that there was simply nothing else she could do.

Ian was still in North Korea. The headlines had made a field day out of his arrest, and then the publicity died down until it could be three weeks or longer before any of the news stories would contain any updates, and the ones that did simply restated what they'd already written so many other times. *Ongoing story ... details as they come in ... blah, blah, blah.* In short, nothing that would help Ian and nothing that would give Kennedy any clue as to how he was being treated or mistreated in North Korea.

She'd grown so emotionally numb she could hardly pray for him except for during Grandma Lucy's weekly calls. Kennedy just had to hope that Ian's grandmother and the thousands of people praying for him around the world — or at least who claimed to be praying for him — would make up for whatever she couldn't offer God right now.

Willow had come out earlier in the fall for a three-day girls' weekend, which helped get Kennedy's mind off her own sorrows for a little bit. Over vegan pizza, Willow told her about the first two foster daughters she and Nick had taken in. While they sat getting their hair done, Willow prattled on about the little baby girl her parents had adopted. They even took Carl and Sandy's son Woong to a Red Sox game, where Willow gave Kennedy a rundown on all the plans she and her husband Nick had for their new home in the middle of nowhere, Alaska.

"Once we finish the second story next summer, we can get approved for eight kids total. Then I think we'll be done adding on."

Somehow, it was nice to hear that in certain parts of the world — even places as far away as Copper Lake, Alaska — people were working in their own quiet spheres to help others. Willow and Nick would probably never win an award for the foster care they provided, would probably never get their names plastered all over the news, but Kennedy knew they were living out God's call to love their neighbors as themselves.

Now Willow was back in Copper Lake, where the sun set at three in the afternoon and everything was blanketed in several feet of snow. This would be Kennedy's first

Christmas break in several years without spending at least a little bit of time in Alaska. It would also be the first Christmas with her parents here in the States, so she shouldn't complain. Besides, with Ian celebrating in some North Korean labor camp or jail cell, she couldn't picture it turning into any sort of festive holiday. Grandma Lucy and her friends from church had planned an all-night prayer vigil for Ian in Seattle, and several other churches in other cities across the country were joining forces. Grandma Lucy had invited Kennedy to fly out to Washington after finals were over, and her parents had offered to buy the ticket if she wanted to go and participate.

She told them all she'd think about it. Really, she just couldn't face the fact that she was almost done with an entire semester of school and God hadn't done anything for Ian.

"You still there?" Willow said, interrupting Kennedy's thoughts. "I asked if you want me to stay on the line while you open it or what."

Kennedy didn't know what to do with the package from Grandma Lucy. The Swedish ambassador who had taken on the role of intermediary between the North Koreans and the US government in Ian's case had delivered a private bundle of letters that Ian had written his grandmother. She spent two afternoons making copies so Kennedy could read them too.

Nothing could make its way into the press, but Kennedy was ready to stay out of the spotlight for the rest of her life and didn't need the extra reminders about the importance of privacy.

"I'm not sure," she told Willow, who was still waiting for her answer. "I think maybe I'll take some time off tonight to read them."

If she could bring herself to open to the first page.

"Or maybe I'll wait until I'm ready." Whatever that meant.

Their phone conversation was interrupted by babbling noise in the background. "Listen," Willow said, "I've got to go. I'm watching Rylee while my parents go pick up a new goat in town, and she's determined to dump everything out of the pantry. But call me if you want to talk after you read them, okay? Or if you'd rather they stay personal, that's fine too. Just know that you can call me any time. Seriously."

"I know." Kennedy was thankful to have such a strong and supportive friend. She wished Willow could live a little closer than four time zones away.

She hung up the phone and sat Grandma Lucy's binder on her lap. Maybe it was because these were photocopies. Maybe that's why she didn't feel any magical connection to

Ian while fingering the pages.

Or maybe she was scared to read whatever might come out, terrified that what Ian was suffering was even worse than the torment her own mind conjured up.

She turned to the first page. Uncertainty was worse than anything, wasn't it?

Maybe. Maybe not.

Either way, she was about to find out.

CHAPTER 16

Dear Grandma Lucy, Remember when I first told you I wanted to travel the world? I must have been, what, thirteen? Thirteen going on fifty, like the little twerp I was back in the day.

Well, I told you I wanted to travel the world, and you said God could use me as a missionary. Hey, it sounded good at the time. And you agreed to pray that God would open doors for me to travel.

You and I both know my life took quite a different turn than what you expected, but I've got to hand it to you, Grandma, maybe you prayed too hard on this one for a change.

So I'm sure the Swedish guy's told you by now. I'm here in the good old DPRK. Maybe you've heard it from the news that the North Koreans caught me trying to cross the border ...

Here, several lines were blacked out, and when Kennedy could start reading again, Ian had moved on to an entirely different thought.

Well, say hi to everyone for me, give them my love, all that stuff. And please try not to worry. I mean, compared to what it could be, it's really not that bad. And no, I'm not just saying that because I know this letter's going to get censored. I haven't been too hurt or anything. In fact, I'm starting to feel pretty lazy. Just wish I had my camera here so I could document everything going on.

If you talk to Kennedy, maybe you could pass a message on for me. The Swedish guy (I'm assuming you've met him if you're reading this, but I'm not supposed to include his name here) said she's back in the States now, and you have no idea how much weight that took off my shoulders to hear that.

Anyway, I'm sure you won't mind if I take a few lines here and give them to her. Kennedy, I know this isn't the time or the place for a really deep Define the Relationship talk or anything like that, but I just want you to know that I've been spending all this extra free time I've gotten (thanks to our dear friends in the DPRK) to think long and hard about everything we talked about.

And maybe when I get out of here and find my way back to Cambridge we can pick up where we left off. Or maybe have that Define the Relationship talk. Or maybe just go out for pizza. You have no idea how much I've missed pizza. And clam chowder, of course, in sourdough bread bowls.

Oh. You and Grandma Lucy will both get a kick out of this. I have a dog here. Serious. His name's Rusty. At least that's what I call him. I don't know if he's a stray or what. People around here don't really keep dogs for pets the same way Americans do. Sometimes they have guard dogs, but that's about it. Anyway, Rusty's started hanging around, and when they let me spend time outdoors, he's right there by my side. Good dog. Ugly as you can imagine, but he's ticklish on the right side of his tummy, and his tongue is spotted black. Hope that's a breed issue and not some sign of disease or anything!

Anyway, just thought the two of you would like to know that even way over here on the other end of the world, I've managed to make a friend.

I'll be talking to you soon. Not sure if Mr. Swedish Courier is going to manage to get this to you before Christmas or not, but don't let my being here spoil your holiday fun, all right? And, Grandma, I want you to know that even though I may have ended up on a different faith trajectory than you hoped or expected I would, I'll still remember to sing a few verses of Silent Night *and imagine I'm back at Orchard Grove's candlelight service. And maybe you guys will think of me when you light the candles.*

Remember how fleeting life is, all that sentimental junk.

Okay, that's enough soliloquy for now. Warm hugs to you both.

Yours,

Ian

CHAPTER 17

Kennedy wasn't sure why she'd torture herself. The more of Ian's letters she read, the more certain she was that he was telling her goodbye.

How could God be so unfair? Why would he allow Ian to go through so much horror? If anything, it should have been Kennedy left to suffer in jail. Isn't that how all the martyr stories turned out? With the Christians in prison, singing hymns to God and sharing the gospel with their captors. Not that Kennedy had done either of those things. But still, if God wanted Ian to be saved, why didn't he intervene? Wouldn't a miraculous deliverance from captivity prove to him once and for all that Jesus was real?

Why did God tarry?

And why did she torment herself devouring these letters? Why couldn't she leave them alone? No matter how upset she got picturing Ian in jail, even though he tried to put a positive spin on nearly everything he talked about, she couldn't stop reading. It was past dinnertime now, and she hadn't eaten since her bowl of dry Cheerios at breakfast, but still she read on.

Hey, Grandma, guess what? I have another friend here, and this one's not a canine.

So I'm in a hospital for the time being, which I know sounds like it's all big and bad and serious, but hey, that's one thing you got to hand to the North Koreans. Free health care for all, right? Haha.

Anyway, I'm in this hospital, and one of the doctors speaks a little English, and it's hilarious to hear his questions. One day, he came in and asked why we have such big grocery stores since we all eat at McDonald's anyway.

So yeah, Doc and I are good pals now, and I thought maybe I should say thanks. You know, if you're the one who's been praying for me. Solitary confinement's about as boring as it sounds, and you know how much I like some time to myself every now and then, but I'll take Doc and his questions for the time being.

And, Kennedy, since I assume I can trust Grandma to pass this letter on to you as well, guess who I've been thinking about most lately? I mean, besides you and Grandma Lucy and everyone back home? I find myself thinking about our two-fingered friend more and more. I know there were tons of things about his past he couldn't talk about, but I guess it gives me comfort knowing that if he can come out of a place like this and go on to lead a well-rounded life, hey, maybe there's hope for me.

You and I talked a lot about PTSD and all that stuff, and I guess it's possible I'll have issues like that when I get out of here too, but with your interest in medicine, maybe you could go on to become the cutting-edge doctor in post-traumatic injuries, and then you can earn tons of money and hire me to go around and make a documentary about you and all your research. Hey, a guy's got to have some future plans to look forward to, right? So think about it.

I bet we'd make a pretty decent team.

Doc's standing at the door of my room frowning, which I think means he wants me to put this pen down and answer his questions about America.

Anyway, hugs to you both. And thanks for sending me all those prayers. God knows I need them.

Yours,

Ian

CHAPTER 18

"How many times have you read those by now?" Willow asked Kennedy a few days later when they were catching up on a video chat.

"I don't know," Kennedy answered.

Willow ran her fingers through her fire-red hair, which she'd gotten done while visiting Kennedy in Boston that fall. "Seriously. You can tell me. I won't judge."

"I don't know," she had to repeat.

Willow huffed. "Fine. Then take a guess."

Kennedy shrugged. "Twenty?"

"Dude." Willow turned around to talk to someone off-screen. Kennedy wasn't sure if she was talking to one of her foster kids or her husband.

"Okay," Willow resumed, "so what can you tell me? I mean, I know it's all hush hush and all that stuff, and I don't want you to betray confidentiality or anything, but you know me. I'm the last person to go blabbing to the press. How does he sound? Is he all right? Do you think they're torturing him?"

Kennedy shook her head. "It doesn't sound that bad, but he did mention he's in the hospital."

"Really? For what?"

"Wouldn't say." One of the reasons she'd studied Ian's letters so many times was because she kept trying to read between the lines. Were things far worse than he was letting on? Would he be allowed to write about them if they were? What if he managed to sneak some hidden message into his notes? It was probably a stupid, juvenile thought, but Ian was one of the most intelligent people Kennedy knew. If anyone could manage to slip in some kind of code that would get past the North Korean censors, he could. She'd studied every single dot of every *i*, practically holding a microscope up to each little period and comma to see if there might be any patterns or trends.

She could probably recite half of his letters by heart but still hadn't come up with anything other than what was on the surface.

"Well, can you summarize or read me a little bit of one or anything like that?" Willow asked. "Seriously. I know you've had enough excitement to last you an entire lifetime, but I'm going crazy here. The power was off for the past two days, and our generator decided to stop working. We just got internet up again, and I literally haven't done anything in the past forty-eight hours except feed kids, take care of the animals, and clean up messes. I'm dying of boredom. You've got to help me."

Kennedy glanced at her stack of letters, which were never far from her. Even when she went from class to class, she carried the binder with her. She told herself it was because the contents were confidential and she didn't want them falling into the wrong hands, but really, she clung to them because they were all she had to remind her of Ian.

She'd prayed far more in the past few days than she had all month. Having his letters, seeing his handwriting somehow made his imprisonment feel that much more terrible. And the fact that he wasn't able to tell her how truly awful it was made things even worse. What if his legs were broken? What if they were giving him psychotropic drugs?

That was one of the stories in her martyrs book that bothered her the most. Some pastor in Communist-led Romania had been sent to a psych hospital when he wouldn't give up his faith. The line of reasoning was that anyone who believed in an invisible God must be crazy. While he was there, they pumped him so full of mind-altering drugs he didn't even know who his wife was after he was released.

Well, at least Ian knew who he was. No matter how bad things really were over there, she had his letters to prove that much. Except most of them were several months old. The most recent was from early November. What else had happened to him in the meantime? And when would Grandma Lucy hear from that Swedish guy with more news?

Kennedy had written Ian some letters herself and forwarded them on in case Ian's grandmother found a way to pass them on. She tried to match his positive tone but ended up printing her words out on the computer when her tears kept splashing onto the paper.

Someone started crying in the background, and Willow frowned. "Sorry, but I've got to go. We're having a couple *bona fide* meltdowns here. But we'll catch up soon, I promise. Talk to you later!"

Kennedy sat blinking at the blank screen, thinking about how much had changed. This time last year, she and her roommate were busy giggling about Willow's upcoming wedding. Kennedy and Ian had gone out on a few breakfast dates off campus, but nothing serious had developed between them. Now Willow was raising a house full of foster kids as well as watching over her small herd of goats and other barnyard critters. Kennedy was behind in just about every class with finals only a week away, and Ian was trapped in some North Korean jail cell or hospital or labor camp.

If he was even still alive.

CAPTIVATED

She squeezed her eyes shut and ignored the lump in her throat, wondering how much she'd be willing to give up for a chance to go back to last year when everyone was happy, content, and free.

CHAPTER 19

Dear Kennedy, I'm sure Grandma Lucy doesn't mind sharing her letters, but every once in a while I thought it might be nice to write directly to you. Thankfully, Doc here at the hospital is more than happy to keep me supplied with paper, although you'll have to excuse the sloppy handwriting, as I'm trying to write with an IV in my arm. No, don't get alarmed. I'll let you know if things take a turn for the worse. Promise. I think Doc is just paranoid. Doesn't want to lose the only American patient he's ever had.

You should see how people react seeing my hair for the first time. It's hilarious. I've travelled enough to know it's a pretty uncommon sight, so you'd think I'd be used to it, but the people in North Korea, man. Maybe it's because they're even more cut off ... No, scratch that. I'm sure if I were to go on with my train of thought it would never make it past the censors.

Anyway, Kennedy, I've been dreaming up this letter for you for a couple days now, which sounds a little pathetic, like I don't have anything better to do with myself, but I don't. Doc's not the most lenient of physicians either. Doesn't like to see his patients up and about. It's so bad that now Rusty, you know that old mangy mutt I've befriended, just sits outside my window whining. I think it's been a full week since he's gotten a tummy rub. But the good news is I've had a lot of time to think about what I want to tell you.

Knowing you, you've probably spent the entire fall semester freaking out about me, and I'm not going to blame you for that. If the roles were reversed, you can be certain that I'd be just as worried about you. But seriously, Kennedy, you're almost done with your senior year. Don't let this little plot twist get you too far off track, okay? You're a perfectionist if there ever was one, and you'd never forgive yourself if you didn't finish your last year of undergrad on a high note. Got that?

Of course you do.

It's funny. Now that I've got this paper and I've started this letter, I'm not sure what to say. I mean, I guess there's all the expected, trite stuff like you'll always know how much I care about you, I miss you so much, blah, blah, blah, but that's probably not what you need to hear right now even if it's true (every word). So I guess I'll start talking about what we were always so good talking about in Seoul.

God.

I've been thinking. (Did I mention I have a lot of spare time these days?) And maybe you're worried that I'll take this whole situation and get really mad at God and blame him for letting this happen to me or whatnot, and I can guarantee you that those types of thoughts sometimes cross my mind.

But then I think about other things too. Like what if it had been you detained, and I was the one set free, and how hard would that be for me? And maybe this sounds strange and New Agey and a little spacey and woo-woo for you, but sometimes I'm convinced I can literally feel your prayers. I had this best friend in elementary school. Gabe was his name. Did everything together, and then one summer his family moved away to Seattle. It's pretty typical. I mean, who doesn't move at some point in their growing-up years, right? But this was different. I mean, Gabe and I did everything together. He lived catty-corner to us, and his family had a swimming pool (I nearly drowned in there once, but that's a story for another day), and we rode our bikes all over Orchard Grove, and literally we were closer than brothers.

So he moved away one summer, and of course I was

devastated, but whenever we went over to Seattle for anything, my dad would make it a point to let me stop and see him. The first few times it was great. Then after school started we went again, only Gabe had a new Nintendo and was totally distracted, and he kept talking about these kids on his brand-new soccer team that I didn't even know, and I realized he'd moved on.

I was ticked, and it's a super long, drawn-out story that I don't really have the time to get into right now, but it was Grandma Lucy who came in one night when I threw this major temper tantrum. She took me into her prayer room and told me that it's often hardest for the people who are left behind.

And I have no idea why, but I've thought about that story dozens of times, and it always makes me wonder what it would be like if I were the one back in the States and you were the one here.

Honestly, I don't think I'd be able to do it. I'm just fine here. Literally all I have to do is lie down and sleep a lot and eat what they give me and let Doc give me whatever it is he thinks I need. That's it.

But you ... I mean, I picture you back in Cambridge, and you've got your classes to go to and your grades to keep up, and I'm sure your parents have been freaking out about what happened to you over the summer, so they're probably breathing down your neck, and this whole time you're worrying about me. (Now that I write that, I realize how totally arrogant and full of myself I sound, so you're welcome to save a slap for me if I'm crossing any lines.) But what I'm saying is I don't think I could handle it if our roles were reversed, and I think prayer has a huge part to play in that.

So I've been praying too. And yes, Grandma Lucy, I know this is going to make it to you first since that's what the Swedish guy says, but please don't get your holy-rolling bloomers all in a wad. Yes, I'm trying to pray more (who wouldn't in a place like this?), but that doesn't mean I believe exactly what I used to believe as a little kid. I just don't want to give you any false hopes.

Anyway, back to you, Kennedy. I mean, you never talked a whole lot about prayer and stuff, but I know you do it, and I know it means a lot to you. Heck, you and Grandma Lucy are probably BFFs by now, right? Correct me if I'm wrong, but I'm guessing if she hasn't sent you one of her famous prayer shawls yet, she's making you one for Christmas. Mark my words. (You read that, Grandma? Better get on it if you haven't yet!)

I guess I've been rambling, but that whole story about

Gabe and everything else really boils down to my feeling grateful to you (both of you) for the way you've kept me in your prayers. Last year, I probably wouldn't have thought prayer could seriously do any good whatsoever. Now I'm not as sure, and I'm definitely not going to risk it by asking you to stop. So keep praying for me (and don't fall too behind in your schoolwork no matter how worried you get. I'm fine. Really, I am.)

    Yours,

    Ian

CHAPTER 20

"Hey, you're late!"

Kennedy glanced down at Woong, her pastor's son.

"Good to see you too," she joked.

He shrugged. "We were supposed to start practice five minutes ago, but Mom's in the prayer room with someone. Again."

Kennedy hadn't planned to help out with St. Margaret's Christmas pageant, but after a recent stomach bug hit town, Sandy lost several of her other volunteers and begged Kennedy to step in.

It was probably for the best. Kennedy had hardly set foot off campus in weeks. She tightened her hold on her backpack, where all of Ian's letters were stored in his grandma's binder. She glanced around the sanctuary. "Are all the kids here?"

Woong shrugged again. "Becky's sick. She's home throwing up, and Brian's got the stomach flu, and Grant has a fever."

Good thing Kennedy had brought her Germ-X. She squeezed some onto her hands and did a quick head count. They were short by at least a third of their cast.

"How long you think my mom's gonna be in there?" Woong whined.

"You'd know that better than I would."

He let out a melodramatic sigh. "I can't stand it when she makes us all wait like this. It's an *abomination*." He rolled his eyes dramatically.

Kennedy thought about saying something responsible like *it's not polite to talk about your mother that way,* but she was too tired. "How was school today?"

"I'm homeschooled, remember?"

"I know that. So how was homeschool?"

He shoved his hands in his pockets and stared at the floor. "Mom got all grumpy because I'd been doodling in my language arts workbook, and she told me to do five pages, but I thought she was joking, so I only did two, and she says if I don't catch up, I'll have to work straight through Christmas. Have you ever heard of such a breach in justice?"

Kennedy was thankful for Woong, thankful for the reminder that for some people, having to do a little extra homework over Christmas break was the most they had to worry about.

Just then Sandy bustled in from the side door. "I'm so sorry to keep you all waiting." She clapped her hands together to get everyone's attention. "All right, kids. Come on. You've had enough free time. I hope you used it to warm up your voices."

Woong beckoned Kennedy to come closer, and she leaned down toward him.

"Don't tell Mom she's an abomination, okay? Then she'd get even more grumpy at me."

Kennedy smiled and agreed to his terms even though her mind was thousands of miles away.

Like always.

CHAPTER 21

"Thanks for giving me a few extra days to hand this in." Kennedy was still breathless from her run to her lit professor's office.

"Perhaps next semester you might think of reading the syllabus ahead of time so you'll know what assignments are coming up." Dr. Penn had a thick British accent, which made her sound even more stern and intimidating than she might have otherwise.

Kennedy held out her paper, finally setting it on the desk when her lit professor didn't take it out of her hands.

"I'm sorry. It won't happen again."

Dr. Penn frowned. "Of course it won't. This is the last paper of the semester, and you're not enrolled in any of my classes in the spring."

Kennedy didn't know what else to say. If she hurried back to her dorm, she might be able to finish her research paper for her cellular biology class that was due tomorrow. It wouldn't be the best assignment she'd ever handed in, but at least it wouldn't count as an incomplete.

When her professor didn't say anything else, Kennedy prepared to leave.

"Miss Stern?"

She turned around. "Yes?"

"I'm aware you are on friendly terms with the journalist being held in North Korea, and I wanted to let you know that I hope he's released safe and unharmed."

Kennedy stared at her professor's feet. "Thank you."

"Perhaps focusing more on your assignments instead of worrying about things you cannot control or change will help you find your way through this uncertain time."

Kennedy wasn't entirely sure if she was being given a lecture or a pep talk. She repeated her thanks and hurried outside. Winter had tarried in New England this year, as if time were standing still until Ian's release.

If only.

She glanced at her clock. Kennedy was officially done now with three of her four classes, and if she finished that cell bio paper tonight, she could call it a semester. She'd tried. Even though it had taken nearly daily phone calls from Willow, she'd managed to complete her assignments.

By this time tomorrow, she should be enjoying Christmas break.

Not that there was anything to enjoy with Ian still imprisoned. But at least she had his letters. She tried to imagine how much harder it would be if she hadn't heard from him at all, if they never even confirmed where he was being held. Somehow she knew it was always best to know the truth. Isn't that why she promised herself that once she became a doctor, she'd never lie to her patients?

The truth will set you free.

Grandma Lucy's words still ran through her head months after she and the old woman had started praying together on the phone. Grandma Lucy still wanted Kennedy to fly out to Washington. The candlelight vigil was in three days, and Kennedy hadn't given her answer, citing her upcoming finals as her reason to hesitate. Really, she'd been hoping for some sort of miracle, that Ian would be released before she had to make a decision.

His case was still garnering national attention, even if the new sites didn't find his story to be quite as worthy clickbait as it was when updates were first coming in. Kennedy heard from Grandma Lucy regularly about different politicians who promised to look into Ian's case. One of the biggest roadblocks was that there was no direct relationship between the US and North Korea. Every diplomatic decision had to go through the Swedish embassy who promised to represent

Ian's case as best as they could.

Several US Senators, and even the President himself, had made public statements urging the North Koreans to release Ian, but what good were words? With no incentive, why would anyone in Pyongyang listen to them? It was like a mouse walking up to a tiger and ordering it to share its meal.

Even worse were all the people who would get on Ian's social media page and say things like *sending thoughts and positive wishes your way* or *praying that you come home soon*. Telling someone you would pray for them was all fine and good, but first of all, Ian wouldn't see their posts until he was already free. Second of all, anybody could say a quick prayer or promise to send *positive thoughts*, whatever that meant, but how did it help? Why weren't these people taking the same thirty seconds out of their day to write their senators or email the embassy or find some other way to pressure the right people, people who actually had the clout they needed to get Ian released?

It's not like the US was powerless. Kennedy was no politics expert, but she knew that if Ian had been a senator's kid or related to some high-up military general, he would have been home within a few days of his news story first breaking. It wasn't that the US was helpless to get him out of there. It was just that they didn't think he was worth the effort it would take. Kennedy knew there were probably political nuances she wasn't considering, but that didn't matter. To all the senators and policymakers and embassy workers, Ian was just some random American who happened to get himself in trouble. Most of the public still believed the initial propaganda reports Pyongyang circulated claiming he had illegally crossed their border.

She finally had to get her dad to post a block on some of the worst news websites because the comments were so upsetting.

What did he expect, sneaking into a country that backwards appeared to be the general consensus of the ill-informed American population.

He should have never gone there in the first place. How many times had she cried over comments like that? It was a smokescreen argument if she ever saw one. Instead of asking why a country like North Korea would hold one innocent journalist in solitary confinement or worse, people just remembered the initial headlines and wondered why Ian would have traveled to a country as volatile as North Korea in the first place.

The wind was howling when she reached her dorm, and she hoped that wherever Ian was right now he was warm. She'd grown so tired praying for his release with no apparent impact that instead she was focusing more on his day-to-day comforts. *May he have enough food. May he sleep well at night. May he not feel too lonely. May he be healed of whatever complication landed him in the hospital in the first place.*

Somehow, it was easier to pray for these simple things than to ask God to send Ian home, which would take a miracle. And as the night continued to darken and the temperature continued to drop, it was getting harder and harder for Kennedy to put her hope in miracles.

CHAPTER 22

"Pass me more cornbread, would you, my dear?" Carl said.

Sandy spun the Lazy Susan. "You know, hon, all those carbs aren't the best for your blood sugar levels. Can I get you more salad instead?"

Carl scowled. "The day I want a second helping of salad is the day I'll trade my Charles Spurgeon collection for one of those mega-church prosperity preachers'." He turned to Kennedy. "Could you do me the kindness of passing the cornbread, please?"

From his side of the table, Woong took a noisy gulp of milk.

"Smaller sips, son," Sandy chided. "It's rude to drink that loudly when we have company over."

"Aww," Woong whined. "It's just Kennedy. She's not real company."

Kennedy had to laugh. It was nice of the Lindgrens to invite her over for dinner to celebrate her end of the semester, but if they meant to get her mind off of Ian, their plans so far hadn't turned out all that successfully. She could hardly taste the food Sandy prepared without wondering what Ian was eating and whether he had enough.

"Well, I'm right grateful to you, Kennedy, for stepping in and helping me with those last-minute rehearsals. I think it's turning into a great pageant."

"Yeah," Woong muttered, "except Chuckie Mansfield is refusing to learn his lines on account of him saying that church is for sissies, and anyone who believes the son of God could've come born as a baby is full of ..."

"Woong," Sandy interrupted, "would you please pass Kennedy some more of the cornbread?"

Woong pouted and spun the Lazy Susan so haphazardly it was a wonder the centrifugal force didn't send the dishes flying off.

"So," Carl said, leaning back in his chair, "any word about your reporter friend?"

Sandy widened her eyes and nudged him, not very subtly, but he waved his hand in the air. "Oh, come on now. We all know that's who she's thinking about, so let's stop pretending everything is hunky-dory and actually talk about all the reasons Kennedy has to be worried."

"I'm really not sure now is the best time," Sandy whispered, but Kennedy jumped in before their bickering could grow too out of hand.

"I talked to his grandma earlier today. She says there's now at least twenty-five different cities that are going to participate in the prayer vigil on Thursday."

"That's wonderful news," Sandy breathed.

"Yeah," Carl grumbled, "if you think that somehow holding a candle in your hand like you're a hippie at Woodstock makes God more likely to answer your prayers."

"It's the principle of the thing that matters," Sandy declared at the same time Woong asked, "Dad, what's a hippie? Is it one of those little yappy dogs? Can they really hold candles? Won't they burn their fur off?"

"All I'm saying," Carl insisted, ignoring his son, "is that more often than not these prayer vigils are just big publicity stunts. So let's say five thousand people come together. Or make it ten thousand across the whole nation. I don't care. They light their candles and say a few words, and then they go home to their nice warm houses. Then what? How's any of this helping Kennedy's friend?"

Sandy shot Kennedy an apologetic glance. "It helps, love, because any time people pray, God answers."

"What's stopping people from praying in their own

homes?" he retorted.

"I'm sure they're doing that too," Sandy replied. "But really, sugar, I wonder if maybe we better have this discussion later when ..."

"And that's another thing that bugs me," Carl interrupted. "How many of the people going to these prayer vigils or love-ins or whatever you want to call them are actual Christians, and how many are showing up because it's the cool, progressive thing to do?"

"Prayer is prayer no matter who you are," Sandy insisted.

"Unless you're praying to the devil," Carl replied dryly.

Woong, who had appeared somewhat bored at the conversational turn, sat up in his seat. "Wow, Dad. Do people really pray to the devil? Does that mean if I ask God for something and he doesn't answer, I could turn around and ask ..."

"Woong, honey," Sandy interrupted, "you left your glass right on the edge of the table. You're about to spill and make a mess all over. See what I mean? Too late now. Pass Kennedy some napkins and tell her you're sorry for spilling on her jeans."

"Sorry," Woong mumbled, apparently forgetting the part about passing the napkins.

"I think it's great so many people will be praying for

your friend." Sandy handed Kennedy a towel. "The way I see it, that poor boy needs all the prayer he can get." She shot her husband a glance as if daring him to contradict her.

Carl shrugged. "I don't disagree, at least not in principle. But I'm also not into turning prayer into a big flashy event. What does Jesus say? He tells us to go into our closet, shut the door, and pray to our Father who is unseen. Now, if people want to show up to these prayer vigils and truly ask God's blessing and protection to bring Ian home, well, then I think it's great and time well spent. But if they're just going there because it's the hip thing to do, then I'd just as soon save the energy." He shook his head and muttered, "I still can't see what candles have to do with any of this."

Sandy reached over and grasped Kennedy's hand. "I think it's wonderful, and of course you know that our family is lifting him up every day. Are you still thinking about flying to Washington to be with Ian's family?"

Kennedy was embarrassed that she still didn't have an answer. Her dad thought she should go, but her mom didn't want Kennedy traveling anywhere. Kennedy had been so focused on finishing her schoolwork she wasn't even sure what she wanted.

"And what about diplomacy?" Carl asked, apparently not

finished with his rant against public prayer vigils. "Can you imagine how much more progress could be made if every single one of these candle wavers took the time to petition the government instead of dripping wax all over public streets and holding up traffic?"

Sandy reached out and touched him gently on the forearm. "I think, dear, that some people might be called to take their petitions to the government, but that doesn't mean we should stop taking our petitions to God in the meantime."

Carl let out a loud sigh. "I suppose you're right. And I'm sorry, Kennedy, if I turned your friend's misfortunes into a personal soapbox. I suppose when things look the most desperate, sometimes all we can do is pray."

Sandy straightened up in her chair. "Now, hold on one minute. You're my husband and you're my pastor and you're the head of this family, but you're also dead wrong. Prayer is never a last resort. At least it shouldn't be."

"Of course. That's not what I meant," Carl said, "but I certainly agree with your point. And that, my love" — he leaned over and kissed her noisily on the cheek while Woong grimaced — "is why we make such a good team."

Sandy nodded her head appreciatively and scooted back her chair. "All right then. Who's ready for dessert?"

CHAPTER 23

It took Kennedy several seconds to realize that she was awake at six in the morning because her phone was ringing.

She picked it up. "Dad?"

"Hi, Princess. You awake? Good. There's news about Ian."

She sat up in bed. "There is? What?"

"Good news, we hope. They're sending Hamilton to Pyongyang." He waited as if he expected Kennedy to start squealing and jumping up and down.

"Who?"

"You've got to pay more attention to the news. I'm talking about Barbara Hamilton. The Secretary of State. Apparently, the trip's been planned for quite some time now, but the media's just confirmed that Ian's case is going to be one of the major points of discussion."

"Does that mean he's coming home?"

"Don't get your hopes up too high yet, Kensie girl. You know how these things work. These diplomatic relations are far more complicated than anything you or I could wrap our minds around, but I'll go so far as to say it's certainly a step in the right direction."

"Yeah. It is."

"So, you're all done with finals and all set for us to come pick you up this afternoon? Will you need any help packing up your dorm?"

She shook her head, trying to wake herself up fully. "No, I don't have all that much to bring with me."

"Well, all those prayers you and Ian's grandma are praying, you keep them up, all right? Like I said, I don't want you to set yourself up for disappointment, and I don't want to speculate about anything too prematurely, but I really think this is the big step forward we've all been waiting for."

Kennedy wondered why she didn't feel more excitement. Was her mind still half asleep? Would it just take a little bit more time for her dad's words to sink in?

"One more thing," he added. "I've been up looking at plane tickets, and if we order in the next forty-five minutes, we can get you to Seattle and back for just $249. I really think that's the cheapest we're going to see this time of year."

Kennedy thought over what Carl and Sandy had talked about over dinner last night. Prayer should never be the last resort. They had both agreed on that much at least. The truth was she could pray for Ian anywhere, and she would. But she also liked the idea of gathering with others who were also asking God for the exact same thing. Usually when Kennedy prayed, even for something as serious as Ian's release, her mind wandered after the first few minutes. Maybe this vigil would help her stay focused long enough for it to make a difference.

Maybe God really would bring Ian home.

She swung her legs over the side of her bed, reaching for her socks so she wouldn't have to put her bare feet on the cold floor.

"Yeah, if the tickets are a good deal, let's do it. I'll give Grandma Lucy a call in a little bit and let her know the details."

CHAPTER 24

"Excuse me! Excuse me!"

Kennedy turned around at the sound of footsteps rushing toward her. "Yes?" She glanced at the wiry man with his thick-rimmed glasses and tattered notebook in his shirt pocket.

"Are you Kennedy Stern?"

She nodded tentatively, trying to recall if she was supposed to recognize him or not. He looked too old to be one of her classmates. "Have we met?"

He held out his hand. "No, I'm Eugene from Channel 2. I understand you were close with Ian McAllister and wondered if you had a moment to give me a short statement about Secretary Hamilton's trip to Pyongyang."

A short statement? Well, what could it hurt? "I hope he's brought home safe and sound very soon." There. Was that short enough for him? She kept on walking.

He didn't bother writing anything in his notebook. "Are you going somewhere? You look like you're in a hurry. Can I offer you a lift?"

She shook her head. "I'm just grabbing some breakfast off campus before I head home for Christmas break."

He stepped in front of her so she'd either have to go around him or stop. "And what would you say, Miss Stern, about all the other tens of thousands of political prisoners presumed to be held captive in North Korea? Do you think that just because they aren't American citizens they shouldn't receive the same degree of publicity that Mr. McAllister's case has garnered?"

"I really don't feel qualified to give a statement about that."

He thumbed through some pages on his notebook. "That's odd. It says here your parents worked for years in China and were active in aiding North Korean refugees, so I assumed that you'd have an opinion on the matter."

How had he found that out about her parents? Up until the day they left China, they'd been more than careful to keep their mission work under everyone's radar. Had Kennedy somehow let it slip at any point?

"Well, I can see you're very busy." Eugene's voice was polite, but he looked like the words tasted sour as they came out. "I'm writing a piece on the way Americans get so up in arms about human-rights abuses when they happen to one of our own citizens. But how many people praying or petitioning for Ian McCallister's release have ever spent more than ten seconds worrying about the other political prisoners in North Korea, I wonder? And do high-profile cases like this promote the cause of freedom or just force us to become even more self-centered as a nation? There's a question I'd love to hear your response to."

He pulled out a card. "Give me a text or send me an email if you decide you want to talk about this further. I can't wait to learn what you have to say."

He yanked some keys out of his pocket and took off in the opposite direction, leaving Kennedy alone on the curb and suddenly without any appetite for breakfast whatsoever.

CHAPTER 25

"No, I'm not upset he asked for my opinion," Kennedy tried to explain. "I'm upset because he kind of has a point." She was backstage helping Sandy set up before all the kids arrived for their pageant rehearsal.

Kennedy had spent the day at her parents' new home in Medford, lounging around, reading books for pleasure again instead of for class, and trying hard to stay calm even with the news about the secretary of state's upcoming trip to Pyongyang. Still, it was different than when she'd usually spent her school breaks at the Lindgrens'. She hadn't realized that having her parents in town would also mean seeing less of her pastor and his family.

Sandy propped the manger on the stage. "So, tell me again exactly what it is that you've been thinking over. Because I hate to admit it, sweetie, I'm not sure I understand."

That was probably Kennedy's fault. She'd been flustered by the journalist's remarks all day but hadn't found anyone to talk to until now. "Okay, so his basic question was why is it that when something bad happens to an American, everyone gets so upset, but those same things happen to people from other countries on a regular basis, and people don't seem to really care."

"Well, I can certainly understand his point on one level," Sandy reflected. "It's just like when a little kid gets kidnapped, and terrible as it is when that happens to anyone's family, it does make you wonder why some cases receive more publicity than others."

Kennedy had listened to Willow and Nick talk extensively about this very issue and how children of color who were abducted were far less likely to even get an Amber Alert sent out. At first, Kennedy assumed they were overreacting until Nick jumped online and showed her the statistics.

"But still," Sandy went on, "I don't think it's necessarily something to get worked up over. Maybe just something to be aware of. Here's an example. You remember that Christian woman from the Middle East who was given a life sentence for breaking her country's blasphemy laws?"

Kennedy nodded. Carl had mentioned the case several times from the pulpit.

"Well, as it turns out, there are more than two dozen Christians in that same country with that same sentence. But she's the only one most of us have heard about. Does that sound fair to you?"

Kennedy glanced around, as if she might find the answer on the walls of St. Margaret's sanctuary. "I guess not."

"Why?" Sandy asked pointedly.

"Because there are so many others too." Kennedy realized how immature the words sounded as soon as they left her mouth.

Sandy pulled out some shepherd staffs. "Well, here's how I see it. Let's say I read a news report about fifty Christians imprisoned for serving Christ in some specific nation, let's say somewhere in the Middle East. And that story reminds me to pray for them, so I do. But then the next day, I might not think about it so much. Sure, if that news article comes to mind again or I read something else similar, I'll remember to pray, but that's probably about all that would happen.

"Now, let's say I read a story with a picture of a woman who's at least in the ballpark range of my age (give or take), and it talks about the difficult time her kids are having with her in jail, and her husband is begging everyone to pray for her release. I hear about it in the news, I know her name, and I know thousands or tens of thousands or hundreds of thousands of believers are joining with me in prayer for that specific woman. How does that sound?"

"It sounds unfair to the other Christians who don't have that kind of support."

Sandy frowned. "I suppose that's one way to look at it. But now let's think. Let's say we've got fifty thousand people all praying for this one woman. And let's say ten percent, or if you want to be even more conservative let's say that five percent, of them go on to pray for that country in general. Or maybe they pray for the entire Middle East or the whole Muslim world. Is that going to make a difference?"

"I suppose so."

"So here's how I see it, hon. You and me, we're made to be in relationships, right? For example, I'm called to be a friend and an encouragement to the folks at St. Margaret's Church. That doesn't mean I'm supposed to find every single hurting person on the East Coast and reach out to them, because that just wouldn't be possible, would it? So instead of feeling guilty that I can only focus on a few individuals when there are so many others out there in need of God's comfort and encouragement, I just tell God I'm ready to serve who he puts in my way today.

"It's the same with praying for others, least as far as I see it. I may spend ten minutes a day praying for that poor woman imprisoned for her faith because I've seen her face.

I know her name. I remember her story. But while I'm praying for her, I can also pray for her entire country to open up to the gospel, can't I? And I can pray for those in jail with her even if I don't know all their stories as well. I guess what I'm saying is that humans will often make any excuse they can for not praying like they should. Some of them will say things like *it's not right for me to only pray about this one person when so many other people are going through terrible things.*

"Let me give you an example. Back when Woong was so sick, remember? I can guarantee you I was praying for my son to be healed more than anything. Now, would it make sense for you or someone else to come up to me and try to make me feel guilty for praying for Woong when thousands of other kids across the globe were suffering from his illness or something even worse?"

"But you're his mom," Kennedy insisted. "That makes it different because it's personal."

"That's what I'm saying. Prayer should be personal. The way I see it, the more personal it is, the better. Let me tell you a story. Back when I was about your age, I would get this newsletter that shared stories of Christians being persecuted around the world. I'd gotten this publication for years and did my best to pray for each and every Christian I read about who was suffering for their faith. But it's like I said earlier. I prayed about them when I read their stories, and then most of the time I just forgot.

"Well, then one day I read a story about a young woman who was my age. And she had a little nursing daughter who was the same age as my baby, too. And her husband kicked her out of the house when he found out she was a Christian, and that's not the end of it. He was so mad, he took that baby, and … Well, I don't want to depress you with the horrible details. But this little baby, who hadn't done anything other than be born to a woman who happened to believe that Jesus is the Way, the Truth, and the Life, ended up suffering some pretty severe brain damage and died because the hospital doctor refused to provide assistance when he heard about the circumstances of the injuries. And let me tell you, that's the first time I've cried over a story about someone I never met. And the reason I cried was because I had a baby that same age, and I knew that could have been me left to forgive my husband for doing something so terrible. And I prayed for that mother by name every day for years because her story stayed with me. Now, that wouldn't have happened if I'd just read some general report about how wives in such and such a country are sometimes kicked out of their homes when they convert. Understand?"

"I suppose. But don't you think it's sometimes manipulative?"

Sandy stared as if she didn't understand the word. "Is what manipulative, sugar?"

"The way they tell these stories just to make you feel bad."

"Feel bad?" Sandy let out a chuckle. "Honey, we're members of the body of Christ, remember? When one part suffers, all the other parts are supposed to suffer with it. I don't see that as manipulation. I see that as us fulfilling our call to remember those in prison as if we ourselves were suffering with them like it tells us to do in the book of Hebrews."

Just then Woong ran up. "Mom! Mom! You've gotta come quick. Becky and me were in the little kids' room even though I know we're way too old to play in there. I didn't mean to but I got Play-Doh stuck in her hair, so I went to help her clean up in the sink, but one of them springy curls of hers got stuck in the drain."

"Oh, my," Sandy breathed. "Is she hurt?"

"No, but she's wicked mad and says she never wants to play with me no more. Can you come help?"

"Of course I can." She stood up and looked at Kennedy. "Well, I suppose it's time to get ready for rehearsal, isn't it?"

CHAPTER 26

The pageant practice that night was like a scene out of a bad family sitcom. Woong's friend Becky spent the first half of the rehearsal crying because her hair had gotten so tangled Sandy had to cut some of it off. Woong was sulking because she refused to tell him she forgave him.

Finally the night was over, and Kennedy was waiting for Sandy to finish locking the church up before heading back to her parents'. Usually, she looked forward to Christmas break as a chance to relax, but between packing up her dorm room, shopping with her mom for new furniture for the guest bedroom, and helping Sandy tonight at the rehearsal, she hadn't had a moment to herself. And tomorrow she'd fly out first thing to Washington to meet Ian's grandmother for the prayer vigil.

"Hello?"

Kennedy glanced up at the familiar voice. It was Hannah, one of the North Korean refugees Kennedy's parents had taken in years ago in China. She and her husband were now in Cambridge, where he was the pastor of St. Margaret's Korean-speaking sister church.

Kennedy gave Hannah a hug. She felt guilty for not having spent more time with her. Hannah and Simon had adopted a little girl earlier in the year, and Kennedy hadn't even met her yet.

"So this is little Emily?" Kennedy had never been all that good with children, let alone ones this little. She didn't want to insult the child by speaking in that silly, high-pitched baby voice, but she did her best to smile at the bundled-up infant.

Hannah was beaming. "Yes, isn't she perfect? I still thank God every single day for completing our family like this."

Kennedy didn't know how to respond. She thought she remembered her parents mentioning something about how Hannah struggled to conceive but couldn't recall any details.

"Is Sandy still here?" Hannah asked. "She told me to stop by to pick up some tablecloths we could use for our church's craft bazaar, but I've been running late."

"She's here somewhere." Kennedy glanced around. "I'm not sure what she's doing. But I can show you where they keep the tablecloths."

"That would be wonderful."

Kennedy still couldn't explain why she felt so uncomfortable. Maybe because when they'd lived together in Yanji, Hannah was such a super-saint. Kennedy had certainly grown in her walk with the Lord over the past three and a half years at Harvard, but she would never measure up to someone like Hannah.

"I hear you're leaving for Washington soon. Is that right?" Hannah asked as she followed Kennedy down the stairs to St. Margaret's kitchen.

"Yeah, I fly out tomorrow."

"I heard Pastor Carl mention something about an update. Did you hear anything about your friend?"

Kennedy nodded. "The Secretary of State's scheduled to visit Pyongyang. Some people think it ..." She stopped herself. There was nothing more painful than shattered hopes. "It might mean progress, but there's really no way to know for sure," she concluded with a shrug.

"I hope you know Simon and I and our whole church family are praying for your friend and his safe return."

Kennedy ignored the way her throat tightened and instead mumbled her thanks.

"It must be hard for you, not knowing if he's okay," Hannah remarked.

Kennedy sighed. "Yeah, it's hard." If anyone could understand what she was going through, it was Hannah. She and Simon had been imprisoned in North Korea before escaping to Kennedy's parents' in Yanji.

Hannah reached out and touched her shoulder. "The promising news is God is watching out for him, right? Just like he did for Simon and me so many years ago. If he could help us find healing and peace after everything we went through, I know he can do the same for your friend."

Kennedy opened the door to the linen closet and stared at the stacks of tablecloths, all organized by size and color. "Yeah, but you two were Christians."

Hannah nodded. "That's true. But suffering is suffering no matter what you believe."

Kennedy wondered if she hadn't expressed herself clearly enough. "That's not quite it. I mean, you and Simon had a lot to endure, but God helped you through it, so it couldn't be all that bad."

Hannah stared at her, and Kennedy felt the need to rush ahead into a lengthier explanation. "I'm not trying to make light of what you went through, but with God shielding you from the worst of the pain ..."

"What did you say?" A flicker of fire lit Hannah's eyes, an intensity Kennedy had never known in her.

"I'm sorry. I didn't mean it like that," she stammered. "But wasn't it sort of like that? In a way?"

"Like what?" Hannah repositioned the pacifier that had

fallen out of her daughter's mouth. She didn't look angry, but Kennedy thought her hand trembled slightly.

Kennedy realized she had absolutely no idea what she was talking about, but she still couldn't stop herself from trying to cover over whatever blunders or mistakes she had already made. "I guess, it's just that I've been reading this book about persecution, and all the believers talk about how when they're being interrogated or beat up or things like that, they describe this Holy Spirit bubble that kept them protected from it all."

Whatever anger or intensity had passed over Hannah, it was gone now and she let out a bright, musical laugh.

Kennedy shut her mouth before she tried to make an even more convoluted explanation.

"I'm sorry for laughing," Hannah finally breathed, "and I certainly don't mean to be rude to you or the author of that book, but honestly, that's one of the silliest things I've ever heard."

Kennedy blinked, uncertain what she was supposed to say or do next. "I don't see what's so funny," she finally confessed. After hearing even a fraction of what Hannah and Simon had gone through before making it to the States, she couldn't understand how anything about that time could induce such a jocular reaction.

"Okay." Hannah wiped her cheeks and tried to make her expression look more serious. "I can't pretend to speak for other believers who have endured persecution, but I can assure you that suffering is quite real."

"I know that," Kennedy was quick to assure her. "But I just thought ..."

"That maybe because we were suffering for God he would make it a little less painful?" Hannah finished for her.

Kennedy tried not to grimace while Hannah wiped some snot off her daughter's nose with her sleeve.

"I'm sure he can do that, and I'm sure he sometimes does," Hannah went on, "but when I was in jail, when I was suffering, it was just as real and just as painful as it would have been for any other prisoner in my situation. And like I said, I know God sometimes does protect his children so they don't feel the pain, but supernatural protection isn't promised or guaranteed. I know the kind of books you're talking about, by the way. And although I'm glad they exist to bring awareness about persecution worldwide, I think they can also be dangerous if they're teaching others that believers are immune from pain just because they're being persecuted for Christ. In fact, it's the opposite that's true, which is why they need our prayers so desperately."

Kennedy pretended to be busy pulling out some

tablecloths even though she had no idea what size or color or quantity Hannah needed.

"Oh, there you are," Sandy called out as she bustled down the stairs. "Hannah, I'm so glad you came. I nearly forgot you were on your way over. Are you finding everything?"

Hannah glanced at Kennedy with a smile that clearly told her whatever blunders or false assumptions she'd made were forgiven. Sandy bustled around the linen closet pulling just about everything out, and Kennedy waited patiently for the two women to finish up so she could catch a ride with Sandy back home to her parents' house.

CHAPTER 27

"All right, Kensie girl. You've got your ID on you, right? And you have your phone charger? I don't want your batteries dying on you while you're in Washington."

Kennedy leaned her head against the car window. Five o'clock was too early for anyone to be awake, let alone on the road.

"We're making good time." Her dad, who hadn't worn a watch in years, still glanced at his wrist out of habit. "Do you have some cash to buy breakfast at the airport, or did you grab something from home?"

"I have a granola bar and some trail mix, but I've got my wallet in case I get hungry."

He frowned. "Well, you know airport food is a racket. I can stop by a drive-through on the way if you want."

"I'll be fine." As long as she didn't have to engage in any deep or meaningful discussion while she waited for her brain to wake up.

"I want you to call me when you land in Seattle, all right?

And then send me a text when you get to Ian's grandma's house. Where'd you say she lives?"

"Orchard Grove."

"Never heard of it," her dad remarked.

Kennedy remained silent.

He reached over and patted her knee like he had when she was seven years old. "You ready, kiddo?"

She turned to look out her window so he couldn't see her roll her eyes. "I'm fine."

"Been a tough few months for you, hasn't it?"

"You could put it that way," she mumbled. What did he think? That five in the morning was a good time for a heavy heart-to-heart?

"I'm glad you'll be with Ian's family. I think it will be good for you. And I'm sure you'll be checking the news, but I'll let you know if I hear any updates about Secretary Hamilton's trip. I just want you to remember ..." He sighed and didn't complete his thought.

"Remember what?" What was this? A guessing game where she had to try to read his mind and fill in the blanks?

"Oh, it's probably nothing. I was just thinking about Ian. If he comes home, you know he's probably not going to be the same person."

"What's that supposed to mean?" she demanded, even

though she knew exactly what her dad was trying to tell her.

"What I'm saying is that as difficult as these past few months have been for him, trauma like that's not something you just jump back from overnight."

What did he think? That Kennedy hadn't experienced her share of trauma since she first arrived at Harvard? Getting kidnapped, being stalked, standing fifteen feet away from a lunatic who blew himself up with a homemade bomb ... Should she start listing out all that she'd gone through? Sure, she was different. She was changed. But at her core, she was still the same Kennedy who first arrived at Harvard University three and a half years ago.

It would be the same with Ian. Yes, he'd gone through some unimaginable suffering. But if he was set free — no, *once* he was set free — he would still be the same person.

Wouldn't he?

"Some people who suffer trauma become withdrawn. Depressed. They might lash out at the people closest to them ..."

"All right, I get it," she snapped. What was he thinking? Did he seriously believe that now was the appropriate time for one of his WebMD recitations?

What was he trying to scare her away from? From ever wanting to see Ian again? Insinuating that even if he ever did return to the States, he'd be a completely different man than the one she'd fallen in love with last summer?

Prey on her worst fears by telling her things she already worried about?

He cleared his throat. "I just don't want to see you get hurt, Princess."

Yeah, Kennedy thought to herself. *You and me both.*

CHAPTER 28

"I haven't stopped praying for you since the moment you got on your plane this morning."

Kennedy accepted the old woman's hug and figured that Grandma Lucy was probably being more literal than figurative.

"My niece Connie is waiting to drive us home. You ready to visit Orchard Grove?"

Kennedy nodded. She had forgotten how short Grandma Lucy was. "It's so good to see you."

Two Christmases ago, both Kennedy and Grandma Lucy had been passengers aboard the same flight. At the time, she never would have guessed that she'd one day end up dating the woman's grandson.

"You have no idea what it means to have you here joining us for the prayer vigil." Grandma Lucy led Kennedy out of the Seattle airport. "I'm so thankful the Lord gave you peace in your heart about coming all the way out here. I was praying about that, you know."

Kennedy was certain she had. Based on her own interactions with Grandma Lucy and coupled with everything Ian told her, Kennedy had the feeling she was walking beside the most prayerful woman she'd ever met or ever would.

"You'll like the farm," Grandma Lucy was saying as she led her to a red car parked by the curb. "We have goats and the cutest little gift shop with soaps and lotions and I'm just so pleased you came out here. I was telling Connie the other day how blessed I feel in my spirit about your visit. I truly sense God's favor." She reached out and gave Kennedy's hand a squeeze. Her skin was surprisingly soft for someone that old and wrinkly.

"Now, listen to me," she sighed, "prattling on while you must be so tired. She released Kennedy's hand and instead put her palm flat against Kennedy's forehead and started to pray right there on the curb. "God, precious Redeemer, merciful Savior, comforting Friend, you are the healer of all our sorrows. You neither grow faint nor weary, and you call us to cast all our cares upon you, which is what we're here to do. Thank you for bringing my sweet little friend to come and be a ray of sunshine to me for these next few days. May we be a mutual blessing to one another, Lord, and may your word dwell in us richly in all our conversations. May everything we do and think and say bring glory and honor to your name, mighty Lord of hosts, King of the universe.

"I'm so thankful, Jesus, yes so thankful. First of all, we give you praise that the Secretary of State herself is going to meet with the leaders in Pyongyang. And I know it's no coincidence that her visit is at the exact same time as our prayer vigil. You yourself have told us that where two or three are gathered in your name, there you are in our midst. Just like you did in the days of Peter and Paul, may you open prison doors and set the captives free in the powerful name of Jesus, who forgives all our sins and heals all our diseases and shows us the way we should go and redeems us from sin, hell, and the grave.

"We come before you, two daughters of the King who both love my grandson very much, who are both waiting with eager expectation and hope for the day when you bring about his release, and not just release from his physical captivity, dear Jesus, but release from all the sin and ignorance that have held him captive for so long. Open up his eyes. Show him that you are the Way, the Truth, and the Life and that no one comes to the Father except by the powerful name of Jesus Christ of Nazareth, for there is no other name under heaven given to men by which we must be saved. And so we trust you, dear Lord, to be the author and finisher of my grandson's faith, to complete the good work you began in him so many years ago when he was just a small boy with the simple faith of a child. You promise that nothing can snatch us out of your hands, dear Lord, so that's what we pray for him today. Take his heart of stone and give him instead a heart of flesh. Let these dry bones rise up and praise you because you alone are the King of kings and the Lord of lords, and you alone are worthy of all of our honor and glory and praise."

Grandma Lucy took her hand off Kennedy's forehead, opened the back door of the car, and without so much as an *amen* or any other indication that she'd just spent the past several minutes praying loudly outside the Seattle airport, she leaned into the car and said, "Kennedy, I'd like to introduce you to my niece Connie. She's going to drive us back to Orchard Grove, so you just find room for you and your bags and make yourself comfortable. We've got a long trip ahead of us, so go ahead and nap if you want. Heaven knows that's what I'm planning to do."

CHAPTER 29

Kennedy had never been to Washington before except for some layovers in the Seattle Airport. True to her prediction, Grandma Lucy slept for nearly the entire drive with a handkerchief draped over her face. Ian's aunt was cheerful and talkative, but Kennedy spent most of the trip staring out the window in silence. She had no idea it was so mountainous out here. Light snow fell on the pass, and she drifted in and out of sleep from the hypnotic sight of the snowflakes falling outside.

"Well," Connie breathed after they turned down what at first seemed to be a never-ending driveway, "we're here. Welcome to Safe Anchorage Farm."

While Connie nudged Grandma Lucy awake, Kennedy opened the car door and was immediately greeted by the sound of bleating.

"You just ignore that," Connie told her. "It's our goat Peaches, the drama queen of the herd. I'm sure she thinks she's dying, but the truth is she's old and ornery and pregnant, so you don't pay her no mind." She nudged Grandma Lucy again until the old woman woke up mid-snore.

"We here?"

Connie smiled and nodded. "We're here."

"Thank the Lord." Grandma Lucy stretched her legs when she got out of the car. "Sweet Jesus, you've given me this one body, and I've done what I can to take care of it all these decades, but Lord, I pray that you'd reach down and heal this stiffness in my bones because you know how grumpy I can get when I'm aching, and I know that's not what you want for me."

Kennedy glanced over at Connie in hopes of finding some sort of clue as to what to do next, but Connie just went around and shut Grandma Lucy's door as if the old woman talked to God out loud any minute of the day.

Actually, she probably did. It was something Kennedy would have to get used to.

The goat Peaches bleated again, and if it hadn't been for Connie's reassurances earlier, Kennedy might have thought the animal was getting slaughtered.

"Come on," Connie said, pulling Kennedy's arm and leading her toward a large farm house. "We're so excited to have one of Ian's friends as a guest. I can't wait to show you around."

CHAPTER 30

Kennedy had never met a woman like Connie, who could turn a tour of a two-story farmhouse into a ninety-minute rundown of a century's worth of family history, starting with Grandma Lucy's parents and their ministry in China before the Communist takeover.

When Kennedy mentioned her parents had also served in Asia, Connie clasped her hands together. "Oh, I just knew the two of you would be kindred spirits. She mentions you all the time, you know. Whenever I pass by the prayer room, if it's not Ian I hear her talking about, I can be pretty sure it'll be you."

Kennedy wasn't exactly sure why Grandma Lucy would spend that much time in prayer for her. They hardly knew each other.

"Oh," Connie continued, her voice as animated as the perkiest of flight attendants, "speaking of the prayer room, I've saved the best for last. Are you ready?"

She led Kennedy to a screen door. Putting her finger to

her lips, she beckoned Kennedy forward.

"She's still praying there, so I don't want to bother her," Connie whispered, "but this is where Grandma Lucy spends most of her time."

Kennedy glanced in. Grandma Lucy sat in a rocker. Her back was to the screen so Kennedy couldn't see her face, but her arms were raised heavenward and her voice rang out loudly and clearly.

"Dear Father, King of the ages, the Prince of Peace and the Lord of lords, you are the one who calms my troubled heart. You are the one who comforts me in all my distress. You are the balm of Gilead, the one who tells me that your yoke is easy and your burden is light. Today I confess my fears to you, Lord, and how distressed I'll remain until my grandson acknowledges you as his Lord and Savior."

Kennedy leaned forward. She'd never been great at long or lengthy prayers, but something in her wanted to stay and listen to Grandma Lucy all evening.

"She'll be a while." Connie took Kennedy's hand and led her away.

Kennedy followed reluctantly, and while Connie showed her the antique tea sets in the dining room, Kennedy's ears still strained to catch the echoes of Ian's grandmother as she poured out her heart to God.

CHAPTER 31

"You're a skinny little thing, aren't you?" Connie piled another massive scoop of shepherd's pie onto Kennedy's plate. "Is that how bad dorm food is these days?" She let out a chuckle. "No wonder my pa wouldn't let me go to one of those co-ed schools."

Kennedy wasn't sure if Connie was making a joke or being serious. What she did know was that if she ate another bite of anything, she'd probably burst her stomach.

Connie sat beaming and elbowed her husband, Dennis. "Isn't she a skinny thing?"

Dennis, who had been reading at the table, looked over the top of his newspaper and scowled. "Guess so."

Connie nudged him again. "Remember when I was that petite?" She exploded into chuckles.

Kennedy wasn't exactly sure what was supposed to happen next. She glanced at Grandma Lucy, who looked as if she were about to fall asleep in her chair.

Connie stood up to pour more lemonade into Kennedy's

glass. "Now, don't be shy. You eat everything you want, but be sure to save room because we have some of our famous cinnamon rolls that will be out of the oven soon."

So that's what Kennedy smelled when she came downstairs from the guest room. "This has all been delicious, but I really can't eat another bite."

Connie waved her hand in the air. "Of course you can. You just have to wash it down with more water to make room for it all."

Kennedy moved her food around her plate with her fork. Her head was swimming with the names of Ian's dozens of cousins that Connie had spent the afternoon rattling off. Hopefully there wouldn't be any pop quiz.

Connie hadn't taken her eyes off Kennedy since she refilled her glass. Kennedy brought a forkful of shepherd's pie to her lips.

"Do you like it?" Connie leaned forward in her chair.

"It's wonderful," Kennedy assured her just like she had after the previous two servings.

"Well, you know, my shepherd's pie is one of Ian's favorites. Isn't that right?" Connie nodded toward Grandma Lucy, who still looked more asleep than awake, but Connie didn't seem deterred. "I'm so glad you liked it. I just had to guess. In fact, I kept meaning to ask Ian what foods you ate after we got one of his electronic pieces of mail where he told us he'd met a nice girl in Seoul. You know, we all assumed you were Asian, didn't we, Dennis?" Connie asked her husband, who continued to read. "And then he sent us your picture, and Grandma Lucy was the first to recognize you from that terrible plane trip you both took, isn't that right?" She nudged Grandma Lucy. "And I had to laugh and tell him, *Ian, when you tell us you found a girl in South Korea, you know you've got to spell out that she's white, or we're all going to assume otherwise, know what I mean?*" This time, her question wasn't directed at anyone in particular, and Kennedy kept her focus on her plate.

"And boy, we could tell after those first few pieces of electronic mail that he was really taken with you, couldn't we, Dennis? I remember telling Grandma Lucy, I said, *I think that boy's finally found a woman who'll make him want to settle down once and for all.* Isn't that what I said? Well, of course Ian didn't get into too many details, and I never could make heads or tails of it. Did you two actually meet over there on the other side of the world? Or did you know each other before that?"

Kennedy wished Connie's husband would put down his newspaper or Grandma Lucy would wake up so she wouldn't have to carry on this conversation alone, but since neither one changed their position at the table, she took a deep breath and tried to decide where to start.

"We knew each other in Cambridge, at least a little bit."

A smile lit up Connie's face. It was the same expression Kennedy's mom would get when she was watching one of the cowboys on her sappy farm romance movies telling the heroine how madly in love with her he was.

"So he was your beau before you went over to Asia, is that right?"

Kennedy tried to recall if she had ever heard anyone called a *beau* outside of a historical fiction novel or a centuries-old classic. "Well, we didn't date all that seriously. I mean, we went out a couple times my junior year, but it really wasn't all that much."

Connie shook her head. "You know, dating was so simple when I was a kid. Isn't that right, Dennis? If a boy was interested in you, he made his intentions known, and by the time you'd been out four or five times, you could both assume things were serious, and that was that. Now with Dennis and me, we knew right from the start, didn't we? We knew we had something special between us. That spark, as I guess you young kids might call it today. I don't quite remember if we had a word for it back then. I'm sure we did, but it's probably so outdated by now. But that's how it was for us."

"So how did you meet?" Kennedy asked.

Connie's eyes grew even wider, although a few seconds earlier Kennedy wouldn't have guessed it was possible. She crossed her arms and let out a laugh. "Ours is a story of love at first sight a year delayed. See, Dennis and I were employed in difference sections for the same company, and we just so happened to work right across the hall from each other. Our bosses were friends, and once they took each of their staffs out to a mixed lunch. Dennis's car was closer than mine, so I asked if I could ride with him to the restaurant. Well, it happened to be payday or else I'm not sure our story would have ever turned out the way it did, but I needed to cash my check. So after our luncheon at the restaurant, I asked him if he could make a quick stop at the bank so that I could go and turn my paycheck in. You know, that's how we had to do it in those days. None of this computer banking nonsense.

"And, Dennis, you'll have to correct me if I'm getting the facts wrong, but he said something like, *Oh, that's no problem. I have to drop my check off too.* Well, I happened to find out much later that he didn't even have a checking account, so you can imagine what was on his mind this whole time, except of course I didn't know it back then. I didn't suspect a thing. So we stopped by the bank, and on the way back to the office, he said — and you'll never believe the cheek — he said, *Oh, by the way, it was my birthday last week, and I didn't get a single birthday kiss.* What a line! Right?" She took her cloth napkin and hit her husband's newspaper with it. He turned the page and kept on reading.

"So that's what he said to me, and then, talk about nerve, he asked if I would give him one. I said yes, expecting a nice, sweet, chaste kiss, but nope, that's not what he had in mind, the scoundrel. He really laid one on me. Then he asked me to go to the movies with him that night. We did, and that was that. When I got back home I told these two other guys that I had been dating — nothing too serious since back then it wasn't uncommon to have a couple of beaus at once — I had met the man that I wanted to marry, so thank you very much, but I didn't need to be seeing anyone else. Six weeks later we went to the little chapel and got ourselves hitched. Isn't that right, Dennis? Isn't that how it happened?"

Dennis grunted from behind his paper, and Connie stood up to clear the table.

CHAPTER 32

Given how early Kennedy had woken up coupled with the full day of travel, there was no reason why she shouldn't be sound asleep.

Except for the way that old goat's yelling carried all the way to her room.

She glanced at the clock. Half past ten, which meant one-thirty in East Coast time. She sighed and rolled over. The attic guest room gave her some privacy, but it was drafty and faced the barn, which probably didn't help the noise level from that silly goat. In the morning, Connie planned to take Kennedy milking. Unfortunately, if Kennedy didn't get to sleep soon, she'd be no better than a coma patient when the sun rose and the time came for barn chores.

The bathroom was all the way on the lower level, so Kennedy threw off the crocheted quilts on the bed — Grandma Lucy's prayer blankets — and made her way down the uneven steps to the ground level. Passing by the prayer room, she saw a faint light and peered in.

Grandma Lucy was on the floor, with her forehead resting on the seat of her rocking chair. Kennedy didn't know a whole lot about growing old, but she didn't guess there were too many people Grandma Lucy's age who could still kneel while they prayed.

Sensing this was something of a private moment, she continued walking past on her way to the bathroom, but Grandma Lucy's warbly voice carried through the screen door.

"I want you to know how much I love him, Father God. I want you to know that even though he's a grown man now, he's still that same scared little boy I cared for all those years ago when his poor mama died. And that's how I'll always see him, Lord, and I know you understand, you being the Father of us all. I confess, sweet Jesus, that I worry more for him than a Christian should, but the truth is, sweet Savior, part of me feels guilty, like I should have been praying more fervently for him to be kept safe on all his travels. Like if I'd been faithful, he wouldn't be in this mess he's in. But even the trials he's suffering right now pale in comparison to the torment and the torture that you went through when you died for him on that cross. And so I'm praying Lord, even if you don't save my grandson's body, even if the Secretary isn't able to secure his release, even if he ends up dying battered and scared and all alone, I can accept that, Lord. But don't let him die without knowing you as his Savior and Redeemer. Preserve his life until just like the thief on the cross he admits that you alone are the Son of God and that you alone hold the key to eternal life. I might never see my grandson again on earth, and if that's the way it's going to be, well, I know that not even a sparrow falls to the ground apart from your will. But if you're asking me to spend an eternity separated from this boy I love, well, Lord, you know I'm not one to tell you how to run your universe, but I won't stand for any of that. Not a chance."

Kennedy had heard enough. Too much, really. She felt guilty for eavesdropping and closed herself in the bathroom. Splashing water on her face, she studied her reflection in the mirror. She looked so tired. They say that worry and stress can age you far more effectively than time. If that were the case, she was probably two or three decades older now than she'd been when she started out as a first-year student at Harvard. Yes, her trials had shaped her and matured her and developed her faith, but if she were given the chance, would she willingly walk through any of them again?

It was one of those times where she knew what answer she was supposed to give, which was different than the answer she would give if she were being truly honest with herself.

It was the same thing with Ian, in a way. At first, she had only been asking herself if going out with him was worth the pain of their breakup, but now it was so much more complicated than that. If Kennedy had known how difficult the semester would be with her worrying about Ian, if she had been given the choice to never go with him to South Korea over the summer in the first place, if they had never gotten serious about their relationship and had ended things with those few quick breakfast get-togethers last year, would it be better? Or was it worth the worry? If she had the choice to spare herself all this anxiety and all she had to do was to never start dating Ian in the first place, never develop these feelings she had for him, feelings that had grown even stronger since his imprisonment, what would she have chosen?

And in the end, what did it really matter?

The past couldn't be changed. Neither could her emotions. She splashed water on her face one more time and turned off the bathroom lights.

CHAPTER 33

Kennedy expected to sneak past the prayer room and make her way upstairs undetected, but when she came out of the bathroom, there was Grandma Lucy in the hallway, staring at her.

"I thought you might have a hard time sleeping. Won't you come and sit with me for a spell?" Without another word, she took Kennedy's hand and led her into her private sanctuary, some sort of converted greenhouse with glass walls on all three sides overlooking a perfectly clear night sky. She never saw stars like this in Cambridge.

"Have a seat." Grandma Lucy plunked Kennedy down in an overstuffed loveseat that looked like it must be Connie's age or older. Grandma Lucy pulled up her rocking chair and sat so close to Kennedy that their knees touched.

"Now, child, here we are." Grandma Lucy spoke in an authoritative voice. "Tell me what's troubling you so we can take your burdens and offer them to the Lord as a sweet sacrifice to the one who bears our sorrows."

Kennedy wondered if she would ever get used to the way Grandma Lucy spoke, as if she were some sort of walking Bible concordance.

Talk about what was troubling her? Where should she begin?

"I hear that you and my grandson broke up before your arrest."

Kennedy nodded.

"Let's start there," Grandma Lucy said. "When did God tell you it was time to break up, and how did that act of selfless obedience feel?"

Kennedy stared at her lap. "I don't know that there was any exact moment or anything like that," she began. "We spent the summer together in Seoul, and we had a lot of good discussions about faith. It sounded like he was at least curious enough to question what he'd believed, so I thought if I gave him enough time, he might ... We might end up on the same page. But then the fall came, and I was about to go back to campus, and I realized he still didn't believe in God, and I knew it wouldn't be wise to keep on dating anymore."

Funny how she had broken up with him nearly half a year ago, and this was the first conversation she'd had with anyone about Ian that didn't revolve around his imprisonment.

"The Lord promises to be gracious to us and to pour out

his blessings on us when we follow him, even if the way is painful. Just like Abraham sacrificing Isaac on the altar, you sacrificed this relationship that meant a great deal to you and offered it to the Lord, and I'm convinced that he has smiled on your act of submission and will grant you his mercy and favor."

Well, that sounded fine if you were a walking Bible encyclopedia, but Kennedy couldn't figure out how spending three nights in the Chinese jail and an entire semester worrying sick about someone she cared so deeply for meant that she had somehow earned her way into God's good graces.

"Honestly," she confessed, "it feels more like he's been punishing me for dating an unbeliever to begin with."

Grandma Lucy frowned. "Well, did you have peace in your spirit about it before you agreed to date him?"

Kennedy thought back to that night of their first kiss. They had been talking about Russian literature, and then before she knew what was happening, his lips were on hers, and they spent the rest of their summer as a couple. "Actually, I'm not really sure I knew what I was getting into. It happened sort of fast, you know ..." She stared at Grandma Lucy's slippered feet, hoping the old woman wouldn't think less of her after the admission.

"Well, you won't get a lecture from me. I know how the heart can lead you astray, and I'm the last one to judge based on my own experience."

Kennedy must have looked incredulous, because Grandma Lucy insisted, "It's true. You can ask Connie to tell you the story in the morning if you want. Or better yet," she added with a chuckle, "I better tell you now so you can stick to the short version."

She adjusted the blanket on her lap, which Kennedy assumed was another one of the prayer quilts she had crocheted, and sighed deeply. "My husband and I divorced after the kids were grown. I'm not proud of that fact, but it's there in my past, and Floyd has moved on to glory now anyway, so it's not like I could seek to be reconciled at this point. Although, in the end, I did try. Well, after he was gone, I found myself communicating with a pen pal in Australia, an elderly gentleman who sometimes wrote articles for Prayer Warriors International. Do you know that magazine?"

Kennedy shook her head, although she figured a publication like that would be perfect for Grandma Lucy.

"Well," Grandma Lucy continued, "I took a difference with something he said in one of his articles. He wrote that since God already knows the future, prayer isn't so much meant to change any predetermined event but to draw us into a closer relationship with the Lord. So I wrote back to tell him what a load of hogwash that was. Think about Hezekiah. The king is sick and the prophet Isaiah himself tells him he's about to die, but Hezekiah prays so fervently and so passionately that God changes his mind and adds fifteen years to his life. Now I'm not making that up or putting words in God's mouth. That's exactly what the Scriptures say. So I went back to Harold and asked how dare you imply that our prayers are only meant to give us some sort of do-good award with the Almighty and not a tool God uses to shape all of history? Because I had already determined that if I weren't completely convinced my prayers were going to change the world, well, why bother? And I don't say so flippantly. That's truly the way I thought about it then and the way I still think about it now.

"Before you know it, Harold and I are writing each other letters every week, and next thing he's booked a cruise that's going to be in the Seattle port for a few days and wants to take me out to dinner. Naïve and unsuspecting as I was, I imagined we'd find ourselves facing off across the table from one another, continuing on in our debate. Because he never did manage to change my mind, but I have to admit that he had some pretty solid scriptural basis for his point of view, fatalistic and pessimistic as it may be.

"So imagine my surprise when he shows up at the restaurant with a dozen roses and a pearl necklace he tells me belonged to his late wife. And something I suppose you'll eventually learn about me is I'm a woman of prayer, and I don't typically do anything without taking it before the Lord and getting his opinion on the matter, but it's not like I thought to excuse myself at that restaurant and lock myself in the bathroom stall until God told me whether I should except his flowers and his dead wife's necklace or not.

"Long story short — and here's where Connie can fill you in if you really want all the details and have a couple hours to spare — Harold became my beau."

Kennedy wondered if talking like you were a character in a turn-of-the-century novel was a requirement for living at the Safe Anchorage farmhouse or if she'd pick up the habit by the time she headed back to the East Coast.

"And in the end," Grandma Lucy concluded, "it became clear in a matter of weeks that Harold and I simply weren't meant for one another, and even now I wish I had had the foresight to get up and go into that bathroom and pray before I accepted his little tokens. All that to say I understand that when the heart is concerned, no matter what your age, you might not make the wisest of choices. And I know my grandson. He can be quite a charmer." She fingered her blanket and chuckled. "When he was just a tiny thing, we took him to see the Little Mermaid movie. Then he came home and swore that when he grew up, he was going to make that little redhead his wife. I shouldn't tell you this, but all through high school he had a slew of girls vying for his attention, but he never got too serious with anyone until he and Abby got engaged."

Grandma Lucy looked at Kennedy with so much certainty and familiarity that Kennedy was slightly embarrassed to find herself asking, "Who's Abby?"

Grandma Lucy started fidgeting furiously with her crocheted prayer blanket. "Now, listen to me. Getting my stories all mixed up so I can't remember what I've already told you and what I haven't." She let out an unconvincing laugh. "That's what happens when your brain gets as old as mine. I'm just thankful the dear Lord allows me to keep my head on straight most days."

"Who's Abby?" Kennedy repeated.

Grandma Lucy sighed. "Well, now, I thought since you and Ian were together he would have mentioned her, but I suppose that's not my story to tell. It's his."

How fair was that? Ian might never get out of North Korea, and then what was Kennedy supposed to do?

She thought about pressing the issue but then wondered

if she really wanted to know. If Ian thought it was important to tell her something about his past, he would have, right?

She stood up. "Well, it's late. I should probably head back to bed."

Grandma Lucy made no move as if she were ready to leave her rocking chair. She took Kennedy's hand in hers. "Goodnight, sweet child of the Most High King."

Kennedy smiled at her, wondering if she'd always been this eccentric or if the change had come with age. It was nice to think about something besides Ian and some fiancée he'd never bothered telling her about.

She offered Grandma Lucy one more goodnight, reminding herself that just because Ian had been engaged at some point in the past, it didn't change anything about those wonderful months they'd spent together.

By the time she reached the guest room in the attic, she still wasn't convinced.

CHAPTER 34

Out of all the things she might be upset about, this really should be pretty low on her list.

So her boyfriend had been engaged to another woman and hadn't told her. That just meant it wasn't all that serious.

But how can you be engaged and have that count as *not serious*?

Was it her business? She and Ian weren't even dating anymore. But if he'd been keeping something this big from her that whole time ...

It was stupid to get herself so worked up. She was probably overly tired and wasn't thinking straight. That's all there was to it. So Kennedy wasn't Ian's first girlfriend. Big deal. At his age, she would have seriously wondered what was wrong with him if he hadn't dated other women in the past.

And it wasn't like Kennedy told him about every single guy she'd dated. Well, actually, she had, but that was because she could count all her serious relationships on one finger.

She rolled over in bed. It made sense for her to lose sleep

worrying if Ian was being starved or tortured.

It didn't make sense to be anxious over something this tiny.

So Ian had a past.

Who didn't?

She'd been moving around so much the sheets were tangled up with the blankets. Kennedy had never heard of prayer quilts before. What made a prayer quilt different than any other handmade blanket?

She rubbed her hands over the wool, finding some soothing comfort in the feel of the numerous bumps.

She was overreacting. That was all. If she were talking to her therapist, he'd probably make some suggestion like it was easier for her brain to worry about something relatively common to relationships — a past love that made her feel threatened or vulnerable — than to fixate on something as unfathomable as a man she'd been so close to suffering unthinkable torment in some prison camp or jail cell.

Yeah, that's what it was. Her brain could handle something as petty and universal as jealousy.

Why had she come to Orchard Grove in the first place?

Why couldn't she pray for Ian back home?

She tried thinking over everything she and Grandma Lucy had talked about in the prayer room but had a hard time focusing on anything that came before the mention of some woman named Abby. Didn't they talk about prayer?

And dating?

Grandma Lucy didn't make Kennedy feel bad for seeing Ian in the first place, but the guilt and regrets had been creeping up on her for some time now. Maybe she should have prayed, just like Grandma Lucy said she should have done with that Aussie gentleman who gave her the pearl necklace. It was strange to think of someone Grandma Lucy's age struggling with romance and unruly emotions just like Kennedy did.

And tonight her emotions were especially chaotic.

Okay, Lord, she started to pray. *Maybe I didn't make the wisest of choices by dating Ian in the first place, and if I did something that wasn't pleasing to you, I'm sorry. But now I don't know what to do. I seriously don't know how I can handle another week, let alone another semester, with all this stress about Ian. I worry so much about him I don't sleep, I'm not eating well, and I barely passed my classes last semester. I just can't do this much longer.*

I thought he'd be home by now. I expected you to hear all these prayers from around the world and act. Do something. How hard can it be? You're God. You can do anything.

Don't you want Ian to come home?

Kennedy paused, ruminating over that last thought. Did she want Ian to come home?

Of course she did.

But somewhere in the back of her mind she recalled her dad's warnings.

Some people who suffer trauma become withdrawn. Depressed. They might lash out at the people closest to them.

If he comes home, you know he's probably not going to be the same person.

Well, no surprise there. Who would go through something that awful and then jump back into day-to-day life as if nothing had ever happened?

But was she ready for the changes?

And since she technically wasn't dating him anymore, did it really matter? Maybe he'd come home and wouldn't want anything to do with her. Who knew? Maybe he'd go find that Abby girl and get back together with her.

It shouldn't matter.

But it did.

And she would continue to be stressed and tired and scarcely functional until she learned how to truly surrender her emotions and anxiety and any thoughts or plans about both her future and Ian's to the Lord.

If only she knew how.

CHAPTER 35

"Now, Peaches is a special goat," Connie explained, "and you've got to be real careful when you're milking her because she likes to make a game out of spilling the pail. And you never want to stand directly behind her either, because let me tell you, I've never had a heart attack, thank the good Lord, but I can't imagine it being much more painful than a goat hoof straight to your chest."

She chuckled while cleaning Peaches' udders.

"Is it just the light in here, or is this goat pink?" Kennedy asked.

Connie didn't slow down. "Nope, it's not the light. She's a special one, all right. That's how she got her name. Now you get your hands clean and hand me that bucket."

Kennedy had watched Connie work on two of the other goats already. A few summers earlier, on one of her trips to Alaska, Willow had tried to teach Kennedy how to milk, but she never got the hang of it. So far, today's lesson wasn't shaping up to be any more promising.

"Careful not to squeeze all at once," Connie said. "It's got to be a fluid motion." She reached out her fist and drew milk from an imaginary teat. "There you go," she exclaimed when Peaches produced a small trickle. "Now just watch your aim and see if you can get it in the bucket this time. We'll make a farm girl out of you yet."

Kennedy finally got into her rhythm right as her hand cramped up. Unfortunately, she didn't have nearly as good luck with her left hand, so Connie took over and Kennedy made herself useful helping to get the goats in and out of the milking stand and keeping their grain trough full.

"Did you sleep well last night?" Connie asked while milking a black and white doe. It came no higher than Kennedy's knee but had just as much milk or even more than the animals twice its size.

"It was all right," Kennedy answered tentatively. She was still deciding how to broach a certain subject. Or if it should be broached at all.

"I got up to use the bathroom and ended up spending a little time with Grandma Lucy."

"I bet she took you into her prayer room, didn't she?" Connie asked with a smile.

"Yeah."

"Did you have a good time?"

It was the opening Kennedy had been waiting for. "Yeah, it was all right. We talked and prayed and had some interesting discussions. She told me about her beau from Australia."

Kennedy glanced at Connie's face to make sure she'd pronounced the word right.

Connie broke into a smile. "Oh, is that a story for you."

Kennedy rushed ahead before Connie decided to give her all the details. It wasn't Grandma Lucy's love life she was interested in learning more about.

"She mentioned something else, too, but I was so tired we didn't talk about it much. I was wondering what you could tell me about Ian's old girlfriend Abby, the one he used to be engaged to."

CHAPTER 36

Whereas Grandma Lucy seemed reluctant to talk to Kennedy about something as private as Ian's former love-life, Connie showed no such hesitation.

"Ian was something of a ladies' man in high school," she began. "Always had some girl or other hanging around and at least half a dozen more nursing major crushes on him. I'm not saying he was stringing them along or doing anything untoward. I think he was so bright and charming and intelligent that the girls just fell over themselves around him. But even though he had his fair share of girlfriends, nothing ever got real serious until he went to college. It was at Harvard that he met a girl named Abby. She was pre-law, and he was going into film and journalism, and for as casually as he dated in high school, with him and Abby it was hot and heavy from the get go. Maybe I shouldn't put it that way, since I truly don't know all those details, but he was quite taken with her. Brought her home for Christmas break their very first semester. I told Dennis, he can tell you this too if you ask, but I told Dennis that I thought she'd be the one he was going to settle down with, and everyone else in the family assumed the same. Everyone except Grandma Lucy. And maybe I should have paid more attention then because one thing you learn about Grandma Lucy is she has an uncanny sense of discernment. Once a friend called her up who Grandma Lucy hadn't talked to in years, and the first words out of Grandma Lucy's mouth were, *So you're finally going to become a grandma.* And she was right. Not only that, but this friend of hers only had one child, a daughter that doctors had said for years wouldn't ever be able to conceive, and Grandma Lucy knew from the minute she picked up that phone, or at the very least had a very strong premonition, that this daughter the doctor had declared infertile was now pregnant, and that's exactly what her friend called to tell her. So maybe we all should have paid more attention when Grandma Lucy declared that Abby wasn't the one for Ian."

Connie cocked her head to the side with an expression that made her look like a curious puppy dog. "Come to think of it, I would have thought Ian would have told you this himself."

"No," Kennedy admitted. "He never mentioned it."

Connie shook her head and mumbled, "Men. It's like

pulling teeth getting them to tell you anything."

Kennedy didn't think the comment warranted a response, so she kept quiet and waited for Connie to continue.

"Well, things were going great from what we could tell. In the summer between their junior and senior year, if I remember right, Ian called to tell us that he and Abby were engaged. Cute story too, by the way. People nowadays are so creative in their proposals. Have you noticed that? Back when I was seeing Dennis, there weren't much more to it than a ring, but now it seems like every beau's trying to surprise his girlfriend and then you get the whole thing on video, which was exactly what Ian did. I can dig it out if you want me to. We have it somewhere on DVD." Connie stopped herself. "Well, never mind," she added quickly. "It's been a while since I've gone through those old boxes, and you know DVDs are far less durable than the old videotapes were, so let's just forget about that." She cleared her throat.

"So where was I again?" Connie frowned and stared at her full pail of milk.

"You were talking about the engagement," Kennedy reminded her.

"Oh, that's right. Well, you don't need the details, I'm sure, but anyway, they got engaged and set the date. You know, I never did understand how real long engagements got to be popular with the young crowd these days. When Dennis and I were seeing each other, all you needed time for was to make your dress and fill out all the invitations, but today people are getting engaged and then waiting two or three years before the wedding itself, and I just don't see the point in that at all, but maybe I'm just an old fuddy-duddy who needs to get with the times." She chuckled and picked up the last pail of milk, and they started heading back toward the house.

"Speaking of engagements," she went on, "I have a girlfriend whose daughter was engaged to be married, and they were going to have their wedding six or seven months later — a nice, reasonable amount of time if you ask me — even though like I told you yesterday Dennis and me did it a lot quicker than that, but this friend of mine, her daughter had her heart set on getting married at some fancy chalet or however you say that. I think it's a French word, but I'm not sure. Anyway, the place they wanted was booked for the whole summer, so do you want to guess what they did? They didn't find some other chalet that would have worked just as well, although you don't even want to get me started on my opinion about young folks who choose to get married outdoors instead of in a church and all the guests have to hike to get to the location, which is what this couple was planning. Since they couldn't get the place they wanted that summer, well, they just push the wedding back a whole year. A whole year. Well, now I've gotten myself all sidetracked. Did I finish the story about Ian and Abby? Isn't that what you asked about first of all?"

She stopped on the back porch and wiped her boots on a mat before stepping into the house.

"All you told me was that they got engaged." A small part of Kennedy wasn't sure she should be hearing this story, but if the past few months had taught her anything, it was that the only thing worse than receiving difficult news was not getting any news at all.

Connie carried the pails into the kitchen and pulled out some clean jars and a funnel. "Well, Ian was engaged, and we were all happy for him. Of course this Abby, she was the sweetest thing and smart as a whip, and she and Ian seemed like a perfect match for each other."

"What happened?"

Connie washed her hands and started pouring the goat milk through a filter. "Well, the way Ian explains it is that Abby's mom was none too happy about their relationship. Abby was a lovely Japanese girl, or at least part Japanese, I don't remember if her father was Asian too or just her mother. Well, I don't know if it was prejudice, or maybe she looked down on Ian because he didn't come from a family with any fancy credentials or extra money, but somehow that woman managed to poison her daughter against him so completely that they had a really nasty, messy breakup, and as far as I know, they haven't spoken to each other since." Connie pointed toward the cupboard. "Can you be a dear and pass me down a couple of lids for these jars?"

Kennedy did as she was asked and tried to decide how she felt now that the great mystery was solved. In reality, the whole story seemed a much smaller deal than it had sounded last night. So Ian had been engaged to someone else, it didn't work out, and that was that. On the one hand, she was relieved that she didn't have to worry anymore or make up stories about why Ian wouldn't have told her about this part of his past, but on the other hand, she felt guilty for prying into what wasn't her business and didn't change anything. Whatever had passed between Ian and Abby, it happened years before he and Kennedy met, and now if she ever did see him again, she'd have this awkward burden of knowing something about his past that he hadn't been the one to tell her.

Then again, maybe it didn't matter.

The chances of Ian's ever coming home felt like they were growing asymptotically smaller with every passing day.

CHAPTER 37

"Do you like the meatloaf, dear?" Connie asked at lunch the next day.

Kennedy nodded, even though her appetite had completely deserted her after her dad sent her such a depressing news link. Secretary Hamilton was unable to meet with North Korea's top leadership like she'd been promised. Instead, she'd been driven around Pyongyang with petty officers who lacked the authority to do anything but serve as glorified tour guides.

"You really should eat more," Connie insisted.

The food wasn't bad, although it might have been more palatable if Grandma Lucy hadn't taken such a long time praying before their meal that everything went cold. Oh, well. Kennedy's appetite had been poor all semester. She hated going to the school cafeteria, seeing all the leftover waste and excess that only reminded her of Ian, who must be close to starving if he weren't already.

She tried to force down Connie's meal, which was

actually quite tasty, but her stomach wasn't used to much besides dry Cheerios and Craisins, her dorm room staple.

"I just can't believe how quickly the time has gone," Connie stated, elbowing her husband in the ribs. "Don't you think, Dennis?"

"Huh?" He glanced up from a fishing magazine.

"I said, 'don't you think the time's gone quickly?' Kennedy's going to have to pack soon."

Dennis didn't reply, but Connie was right. In just a few hours, one of the men from Orchard Grove Bible Church would come by to drive Kennedy and Grandma Lucy to Seattle for the prayer vigil. Connie had to stay home with the goats, and since Kennedy was flying out the following morning, it made more sense to spend the night in Seattle rather than drive all the way back out here just to catch a few hours of sleep.

"Do you need an extra suitcase, dear?" Connie asked.

Kennedy shook her head. Even though she was returning to Boston with one of Grandma Lucy's prayer blankets and several trinkets Connie gave her from the farm's little gift shop, she had plenty of space.

Connie let out a contented sigh. "I do declare, it's been so nice having a friend of Ian's with us, hasn't it?" She scooted back her chair. "Well, I suppose I need to get these dishes cleaned up, and then I'll help pack Grandma Lucy a few things for her big trip to Seattle. I'm just so tickled you'll be there praying tonight for Ian, that poor boy."

Connie clasped her hands together by her chest and looked up toward the sky. Kennedy wondered what she had to be so excited about.

Ever since she heard about Secretary Hamilton's failed mission to North Korea, Kennedy got the sickening feeling that tonight's gathering would be less like a prayer vigil for someone who had hope of rescue and more like a memorial service for a man who'd already died.

CHAPTER 38

"Come in, come in." Connie swung open the farmhouse door and embraced the young man with a giant hug. "Scott, this is Ian's good friend Kennedy. Kennedy, I'd like to introduce you to Scott Phillips, who just moved to Orchard Grove from your neck of the woods."

"Actually, I've been here a year," the tall man said, stepping into the farmhouse. He gave Kennedy a smile. "Nice to meet you."

Connie had already given Kennedy the abbreviated version of Scott's entire life story. He'd spent years on the mission field before moving to Orchard Grove and marrying a local girl, and Kennedy figured they could find quite a bit to talk about on the way to Seattle.

"Grandma Lucy!" Connie called out. "Scott's here. Are you ready?"

Grandma Lucy emerged from her prayer room, groaning slightly as she leaned against the wall.

Connie bustled over to help her. "You tired today?" she

asked.

Grandma Lucy paused before making her way down the hall. "No more so than usual, praise the good Lord. And Scott, I hope you don't mind if I just rest my eyes on the drive over. I'm afraid I won't be much company to you on the road."

Scott smiled. "Don't worry about it. Can I help you to the car?" He offered his arm.

Kennedy carried her suitcase and set it in Scott's trunk then turned to say goodbye to Connie. "Thanks for everything. It was really nice getting to know you."

"Well, you take care of yourself now." Connie wiped her cheeks and smiled. "I hope you know that even though I can't make it to Seattle tonight, I'll be praying for Ian more than ever." She leaned in for one last hug that smelled like cinnamon rolls and goat milk and old-lady hair spray all at once.

Kennedy glanced behind Connie's shoulder. "Where's your husband?"

Connie waved her hand in the air. "Don't worry about him. He's probably in the den reading or something, but I'll tell him you said goodbye." She wiped her cheeks again. "Be safe. God bless you." She hurried over to help Grandma Lucy get situated in the back seat, and the old woman was asleep even before Scott made it halfway down the long, winding driveway.

"What'd you think of the goat farm?" he asked as he turned onto the road.

"It was great," Kennedy replied automatically, although she knew she'd need more time than thirty seconds to process everything she'd experienced in the past couple days. For some reason, she'd come out here thinking she would find some sort of connection to Ian. As much as she admired his family, even with their little oddities, she realized now more than ever just how far away from her he really was.

Ian wasn't in Washington.

He was in some jail in North Korea, suffering for crimes he never committed, at the mercy of one of the most horrific, oppressive regimes in recent history.

She thought about the conversation she'd had with Hannah. *When I was in jail, when I was suffering, it was just as real and just as painful as it would have been for any other prisoner in my situation.*

It was a new way of looking at suffering and persecution for sure. Up until she started to really think through it, Kennedy had bought into the whole idea that Christians who were persecuted for their faith were guaranteed some sort of special grace or miraculous power to rejoice in their trials. It seemed like a biblical concept. After all, God did promise to work everything together for good.

But what Kennedy hadn't ever thought about before was that the suffering of persecuted believers was just as real as any other form of suffering on earth.

She thought about her own experiences in college, how many times she'd been forced to walk through terrifying circumstances or come face to face with grief or terror or anxiety. Yes, at certain points she'd been aware of God's presence. She'd experienced the supernatural peace that believers talked about.

But just as often, she'd experienced the despair and fear and darkness. Just because she was a Christian didn't mean she didn't feel the pain or the sorrow as poignantly as anyone else would.

Still, she'd feel better if Ian were a Christian, if she could at least picture him finding some sense of comfort from the Holy Spirit. His collection of letters, which she continued to carry with her nearly everywhere she went, were cheerful, but how much of that was a show so she and Grandma Lucy wouldn't worry so much?

And how selfless did he have to be, Christian or not, to put his own suffering aside in order to make the people he loved feel better?

Kennedy let out her breath.

"You must be tired from traveling so much," Scott commented from the driver's seat.

"Yeah." She chuckled. "I should be used to it, though. My parents were missionaries in China for years, and we traveled all the time."

"I remember Connie saying that." He turned onto Orchard Grove's Main Street and let out a chuckle. "You'll have to forgive me. Or maybe it's her you'll have to forgive, but I already got the rundown of your life story when she made the arrangements for us all to drive together."

Kennedy laughed. "Don't feel bad. I know all about you too."

"Really? What'd she say?"

Kennedy wasn't sure how much she should divulge.

"Come on," he prodded. "Connie's a talker, but she's a perfectly harmless old soul. What did she tell you?"

"Well, I didn't get all the details, but there was something about you meeting a girl online, then moving out and marrying her right away and causing some sort of scandal around town."

He laughed. "Guilty as charged." He pulled his phone out of his pocket. "Here. Go to my home screen and you can see her and our daughter."

Kennedy swiped the screen. "Oh, my goodness. What a tiny baby!"

"That's little Gloria." He was beaming even though his eyes were on the road.

"Connie didn't even mention a baby."

Another laugh. "Yeah, well, Susannah had the unfortunate luck of getting pregnant on our honeymoon and delivering three weeks early, so you can guess what a stir that made in a town like this."

"I bet." Kennedy wasn't exactly sure how she felt about discussing conception dates with a married man she'd just met, so she tried to change the subject. "So you were a missionary? Where did you work?"

"All over. I'm with a group called Kingdom Builders, and we have field offices on six continents. Basically, we're the missionaries to missionaries. We provide encouragement and counseling services to other workers on the field, run quite a few programs for missionary kids ..."

"Really?" Kennedy interrupted. "Like what?"

"Well, we have summer camps set up in various countries. We take kids all the way from K through 12, basically give them what you'd think of as a typical summer camp experience for the week. But in addition to cabins and canoe races and mosquitoes and campfires, we have special discussion groups about some of the unique difficulties you confront as a TCK."

A sense of warmth rushed over Kennedy's whole body. Finally, someone was speaking her language.

Scott glanced over. "You know all about it, I'm sure. You were a third-culture kid yourself."

"Yeah." She let out a chuckle. "It was really hard coming back to the States for college. All through high school, I kept telling myself that once I was back in America, I'd finally feel like I belonged, but I wasn't American enough to fit in here just like I wasn't Chinese enough to fit in there."

"Typical third-culture kid dilemma," Scott remarked. "So tell me. Connie says you've had quite a few close-calls and things since you first came to college. I know she can sometimes tend to exaggerate, but most of the stories sounded really serious. What's up with all that?"

Kennedy glanced at the clock. "How much time have we got?"

CHAPTER 39

They were already halfway up the North Cascades pass when Kennedy finished telling Scott about each of her close calls over the past three and a half years.

He let out a low whistle. "What are the chances of all those things happening to one college student?"

"I know what you mean." How many times had she asked herself that same question?

"You should write a book or something," Scott said. "You could turn it into a whole series. I think readers would love that."

She rolled her eyes. As difficult and dangerous as her life had been, she still couldn't picture anyone wanting to sit down and read about it. "They'd probably get too depressed," she joked. "Or decide it's way too implausible."

He shrugged. "Yeah, maybe. But how are you doing? I mean, you sort of glossed over that time you spent in the Chinese jail."

"It was only three days." Why did her core start

trembling now of all times?

"Three days or three years, that sort of thing is really hard to go through."

"I guess I've been so worried about Ian, I don't really think my time in China was all that bad. Know what I mean?"

He nodded. "For what it's worth, I'm sorry you had to go through that, and I'm sorry for Ian too. I haven't met him, but Grandma Lucy talks about him all the time."

She let out her breath and glanced in the backseat where Grandma Lucy snoozed with a cowboy handkerchief covering her face.

"What is it you do now?" Kennedy asked. "I mean, do you still travel a lot for your mission work and stuff like that?"

"Most of what I do is telecommuting at this point. Home office support. You know, a couple years ago I hated the thought of staying put anywhere, but now that I'm married, and especially now that we have little baby Gloria, there's not anywhere else I'd rather be. I'm glad I'm able to keep working for Kingdom Builders and still support my family."

Kennedy was years away from settling down, but Scott's young bride in the photo hadn't looked any older than she was. She thought about her best friend Willow, married now and helping raise foster kids out in Alaska …

When had everyone around her become an adult?

"Hey," Scott said, "here's something you might be interested in, with your connections in both China and North Korea. I've been asked to prepare a TIM talk for the World Missions Digest podcast."

"What's a TIM talk?"

"*Teaching in Missions.* It's all topical stuff, ways to encourage missionaries and sending churches and basically the global church in general when it comes to the ways we think about and go about and fund world missions. My topic is on persecution myths. I've been working on it for a few weeks now, every night when I'm up late on baby duty."

"What kind of myths are you talking about?"

"Oh, the typical. How we tend to over-glamorize persecution, so we get this sense that anyone suffering for their faith must be some sort of super-Christian. I want to talk about not only the problems with that sort of thinking but how I think it's really stunted church growth. Want to hear my rough outline and give me some feedback?"

Kennedy glanced at the time. They were still at least an hour from Seattle. "Sure."

"All right. One thing I want to bring up is the way people glorify suffering to the point that they'll say things like the

American church needs to be persecuted if we want to become purified. And they'll cite China as if it's some big Christian utopia, but as I'm sure you and your parents already know, persecution has made it so hard to obtain Bibles in China that there might be only one copy of Scripture in a city of a million. Most folks in the west have no idea of all the heresy that can come when people don't have access to God's word.

"My other big problem with that sort of thinking is when we treat persecuted believers like super-Christians, we sort of get this feeling like they're so spiritual and so lucky to be suffering for their faith they don't even need our prayers. Right? Because we want to assume any Christian who suffers for the gospel is automatically going to be protected, so it's not really suffering. But here's how I look at it. Let's say, heaven forbid, you or I get diagnosed with some fatal illness. Now, for some believers, they're going to have a ton of peace and be completely faithful and trust that whatever God has in store for them, it's part of his perfect will. And some of us are going to handle it a lot differently. Same thing with persecution.

"And then there's one other major problem I see with glorifying believers who suffer for their faith, and this is the one I'll focus on most in my TIM talk. We get so enamored with the idea of suffering for the gospel that we've got this horrible persecution complex. I mean, all you have to do is go to one of those watchdog websites that talk about religious freedom in the US, and you'll see it all over the place.

"Someone's not allowed to wear their cross necklace, and all of a sudden we're acting like evangelical Christians are the most hated, marginalized population in the country. Sure, if I were the one making up all the laws, I'd say let them wear their crosses. But then you've got to be prepared to let the Muslims wear their hijabs and the Jews their kippahs and the Sikhs their turbans, and as long as that's not offensive to you, then yeah, let's keep promoting religious freedom.

"But just because someone's not allowed to read their Bible on company time, I don't see how the kingdom of God is going to be advanced when we take these cases to court or we plaster all these fear-mongering headlines meant solely to convince people that Christianity is the most despised religion in the country. That's what I mean when I say we've got a persecution complex, and I think that's dangerous for two reasons. First, it diminishes the very real persecution that Christians around the world do face. Trust me, it's not cute or pretty or glamorous. I've sat in the same room while our India field director told a mother of four that her husband was killed by Hindu extremists. I've visited a ten-year-old boy in North Sudan who was the only surviving member of his family but who suffered so many machete injuries he's going to be permanently disabled. After you see a few dozen instances like this, you tend to not have much sympathy for American Christians who have never seen the inside of a jail cell but who are a little upset because some store decides to say *Happy Holidays* instead of *Merry Christmas.* Not to mention how it makes all Christians sound whiney and petty."

He let out his breath. "Sorry. I get kind of worked up about this."

Kennedy didn't know what to say. How could she argue when he had seen so many things she couldn't even imagine? "It does make the suffering we've got here in the States sound pretty minor in comparison," she admitted.

"Oh, I'm not denying the fact that Christians suffer. It's universal," Scott went on. "Think about your life, for example. Just because someone else on the other side of the world is experiencing a different kind of suffering, that doesn't diminish what you've gone through. I can only imagine how hard it must be for you with your boyfriend in North Korea right now."

"Actually, we broke up right before the arrest."

"Really? Connie didn't mention that part."

"Yeah, it got muddled in all the other news."

"I'm sorry. What happened?"

She let out a heavy sigh. "Well, you know he's not really a Christian even though he was raised in the church, and …"

"And you gave up your relationship because you knew that's what God wanted you to do?" he finished for her.

"Pretty much."

"That's hard."

"Yeah."

"I'm assuming you probably still have strong feelings for him, all that?"

"Pretty much."

"So things would probably be fairly complicated and confusing even if he weren't in jail."

"Pretty much," she repeated.

Scott glanced in the rear-view mirror. "Well, Grandma Lucy's out like a light, and I certainly can't promise to be nearly as eloquent as she would be, but I'd love the opportunity to pray for you if that's something that wouldn't make you too uncomfortable."

"Sure," she replied, although with all the people who'd been praying for her and Ian over the past several months, she wasn't sure how much faith she had that one more prayer was going to change anything.

CHAPTER 40

It was dinnertime when they arrived in Seattle. Scott stopped to grab everyone sub sandwiches and then went to gather on Capitol Hill where Ian's prayer vigil would start in about half an hour.

Kennedy didn't love the idea of being in such a huge crowd. She'd never really gotten over her germaphobia, and getting stuck in that hospital during an epidemic a few years back only exacerbated the issue. She was glad it was winter, so she could wear mittens and cover her mouth and nose with a scarf.

For a short time, she'd considered giving up her plans to become a doctor altogether. In addition to her fear of germs and her hatred of hospitals, she'd kind of flipped out last winter when she had to help Willow deliver a baby in the middle of nowhere. Going to South Korea last summer and seeing the work that Freedom Korea did to help refugees made her rethink her plans even more, especially once the director asked her to intern after graduation.

She had prayed about her decision, and even though she felt called to work in Seoul, she still couldn't give up her dreams of med school altogether, which is why she'd requested the deferment.

It was funny how she'd spent so long worrying over her future, getting anxious about choices she wouldn't have to make for years, but over the past semester, she didn't have the mental energy to worry about anything other than Ian's release. Maybe that was one blessing that came out of this entire ordeal. But couldn't God have taught her to worry less some other way without throwing Ian in a North Korean jail?

Scott helped Grandma Lucy to a podium in front of the growing crowd, where she could sit for the vigil and not have to worry about getting jostled or thrown off balance. He told Kennedy there was room for her on stage too, but she wasn't sure which she feared more — all the germs she'd come into contact with once the crowd numbers swelled or all the eyes that would be staring at her if she took her place up front. She decided to hang out near the stage where she could always make a quick escape if the crowds got too overwhelming, but she wasn't right up there in front of the microphone for everyone to see.

"You doing okay?" Scott asked her after he made sure

Grandma Lucy was comfortable and warm.

"Yeah. It's already quite a turnout, isn't it?"

Scott smiled at her and nodded. "It is. I have a good feeling about tonight. I really think we're about to see God move."

It was a comforting sentiment, but Kennedy's soul was too tired to put much hope in his words.

CHAPTER 41

Kennedy wasn't great at estimating numbers, but Scott said there were at least a thousand or more people by the time the prayer vigil started. Christian leaders from around the Seattle area took turns at the microphone, and in between their prayers a hipster-looking guitar player in skinny jeans led the crowd in a few songs Kennedy hardly knew.

Scott was one of the ones scheduled to speak, and he gave what Kennedy figured must be some sort of dress rehearsal for his upcoming TIM talk on missions and persecution. Kennedy wasn't sure how appropriate it was to talk about Christian martyrs at an event like this, especially since as far as everyone knew, Ian was still alive, and it's hard to become a martyr for a faith you'd rejected years ago.

She sighed. Maybe she shouldn't be so pessimistic, but she'd been hoping for something more than this. Something deeper. For God to reach into her heart and speak to her personally, to promise her that she'd see Ian again or give her some other sign or comfort to hold onto. All the prayers and songs were nice, but they didn't change the fact that Ian was still so far from home.

What had he already gone through? Was he still in the hospital? What were they treating him for anyway? Was he in one of the infamous prison camps now? Or what about solitary confinement? Kennedy had only been in that Chinese jail for three days, and she had an inquisitive guard to talk to by day and Ian at night. Even then the darkness and fear and oppression had nearly driven her to despair. How much worse would it be for Ian, stuck there for so many months, without even the hope in Christ that Kennedy had?

In one of his letters, he mentioned feeling her prayers for him, but in the past few weeks, she'd grown so tired and discouraged most of her prayers were nothing more than complaining to God about the situation. What did that mean for Ian? Did he sense the change when Kennedy stopped praying for him so fervently? She had always believed in the supernatural power of prayer, but as a biology student she also figured there was some scientific basis for a lot of it as well.

Praying — no matter what your religion — had been shown to reduce stress, optimize health, and decrease anxiety. In her mind, that just gave scientific backing for what she already knew from the Bible to be true.

It made perfect sense when you were talking about praying for yourself. But what about praying for someone else? What about praying for people who didn't even know they were being prayed for?

Would the results be as beneficial?

Could researchers propose some sort of scientific explanation, or was it all supernatural?

And in the end, did it matter? If prayer worked, prayer worked, right?

But she still felt guilty for the way her petitions for Ian had tapered off lately. Thankfully he still had his grandma to pray for him. That woman would never waver in her faith. Grandma Lucy's body swayed during Scott's closing prayer, then she stood up and shuffled toward him. Kennedy was afraid she might fall and was about to jump on the stage to support her, but Grandma Lucy reached Scott in time and told him, "I'd like to say a few words if I may."

Scott smiled. "Of course. Shall I introduce you?" After she nodded, he spoke directly to the crowd. "This is Ian's grandmother."

The introduction was met by soft murmurs and muffled clapping. Grandma Lucy took the mic.

"Thank you. Thank you all for being here. I can't tell you just how pleased I am to see so many of you coming out here to honor my grandson with your prayers and support, and I'd like to remind you of the passage from Scripture that says if anyone agrees anything in the powerful name of Jesus, it will be granted to us. There is power in agreement, power when we come together and with one spirit raise up our voices and petition the King of the universe to hear our prayers and work justice on behalf of the oppressed.

"My grandson is suffering tonight in a country where thousands have lost their lives. This is a country of darkness, both literal and spiritual, but tonight, I want to ask you to do something special. I don't want you to just focus on my grandson. Heaven knows he needs our prayers, and there will be plenty of time for that. But let's not lose sight of the grand scheme, either. The grand scheme is that not just one American but tens of thousands and maybe more prisoners are languishing behind North Korea's closed gates. They are torn from their families. They are tortured and starved. Some of them are our brothers and sisters in Christ but others have never heard the name of Jesus.

"Now, I'm not going to pretend that these months worrying for my grandson have been easy, but I do want to stand here today and tell you that the time of fellowship I've had with the Lord while praying for my grandson has been sweet and refreshing to this old weary soul of mine. Before his arrest, my mind was weak. Doctors said it was dementia. But learning to pray so steadfastly for my grandson has proven to be all the cure I need. My mind is sharp, and I know this is God's gift to me and nothing medical science can explain. Not only that, but God has used this terrible situation to teach me to pray more deeply for the people in North Korea. It would be selfish of me to spend all my time praying for Ian when so many thousands of others are suffering with no one to pray for them, with no one in the free world who even knows their names. I admit that at first it felt overwhelming. How could I pray for an entire nation of people when my heart was so riddled with terror and anxiety on behalf of my own flesh and blood? But then I told the Lord that if he wants to use my grandson's imprisonment to teach this old dog one last trick, to teach me to pray for the people of North Korea in a way that I've never prayed for anybody or anything before, well who was I to argue with the Almighty?

"And so I prayed. Each time I prayed for my grandson, I remembered to pray for his guards too. And then I got to thinking that those guards have families, and many of them are just doing what they're doing because if they don't, their families could starve, and I felt compassion growing in my heart for this entire people group because even those who aren't in prisons like my grandson are still held in captivity, slaves to a dictator, slaves to darkness. And so I prayed. Dear Lord, I prayed, open those floodgates of heaven and pour your light onto the people of North Korea. Shower your grace upon them so they can see you are the one true God and with you there is salvation for their souls and forgiveness of their sins. Tear through the veil that holds them captive, Father God, for you see them, these sheep without a shepherd, these orphan souls who have never known the truth about their divine Father. Reach down, Lord, and see their misery. Mark their tears on your scroll, and heal them from their darkness and their pain and their despair. Heal them from their ignorance, and shatter those chains."

Grandma Lucy emphasized each individual word.

"Let them be free," she continued, "and let them know that with you there is hope. With you there is salvation for their souls. And with you there is a reason to live and exist. You created these children to worship you, so show them who you are. Break down the walls that hold this entire nation in captivity. Rip off those blinders that have kept generations in darkness. Father God, I believe that you are doing something new in the nation of North Korea. I believe that the day is coming when every single prisoner will be set free from their chains, and I'm not just talking about the ones like my grandson, Lord. There's a spiritual bondage that's an even crueler fate than what Ian suffers today. But I believe and I declare that you are the God of North Korea, that you will reign in that nation once more. That the darkness will have to give way to the glorious light of the one true King. That whatever idolatry has been set up will be shattered, that whatever demonic influence is holding this people captive will be slaughtered and destroyed in the name of Jesus. It's a war, Father God, which is why we declare you as the conqueror. This isn't a battle we can fight with politics or diplomacy. This is a war that can only be won by the blood of Jesus Christ, the blood that was shed on the cross so that the people living in North Korea today would know the truth that you are their Savior and their healer, their creator and their king.

"And so I speak to the darkness tonight, sweet merciful Savior. I speak to the darkness that is hovering over North Korea, and I tell it to be gone. It has no place anymore. I speak to the forces of evil that have their talons entrenched in the ruling class of North Korea, and I command them to flee before Jesus Christ, who conquered death, hell, and the grave and who has already declared victory in North Korea."

A low grumble rose from the crowd, Christians breaking into applause or murmurs of agreement, but Grandma Lucy only raised her voice and spoke even more boldly into the microphone, her words carrying above the rumble of the masses.

"The devil thinks that North Korea is his little playground, and that's what it's been, but no longer. From this moment on, we declare victory. We set up Jesus as the high and sovereign King over North Korea, over every law, over every politician, over every government official, from the lowly schoolteacher to the Supreme Leader himself, and we proclaim that there is no authority under heaven that has not been established by God and that the same God who sets up kings and deposes them will have his way in North Korea. We declare that freedom will reign, and the blood that flowed down from Jesus's nail-pierced hands when he hung and died on that cross is the same blood that right now covers North Korea and washes away the sins of its past. All the massacres, all the purges, all the murder and strife and starvation and sickness and despair, we proclaim these healed by the blood of Jesus, and not only that, but we speak redemption. We don't ask simply for a North Korea where oppression is ceased. We ask for a North Korea where every single individual will encounter the one true God, will acknowledge him the Savior of their lives, to repent, to be forgiven of their sins. We pray for the land itself, the land of

North Korea that is flowing with so much blood, to be cleansed so that the ground itself will become a haven, not simply of political freedom, but of spiritual worship, that the men and women and children there, yes Lord even those alive today, will one day bow down and worship you and exalt you as King."

Grandma Lucy reached out and took Scott's arm, and he led her on wobbly legs back to her seat. Kennedy wasn't sure what had just happened. She'd need time to think about it before she could articulate her thoughts even to herself, but she realized Grandma Lucy's prayer had done more than just inspire the crowd to pray for North Korea.

It had healed something in her soul, a woundedness Kennedy hadn't even known existed. It was like having a sore throat for weeks until she scarcely noticed it anymore, but then one day she woke up and it was gone, and she realized how much better she felt.

She didn't know what it was, but something had changed in her spirit. Something had been fixed, and now that she knew what it felt like to no longer be so broken, she prayed that she would never have to go back to that fear and anxiety she had lived with until now.

After helping her back to her seat, Scott returned to the podium, holding his cell phone and smiling broadly. "I don't know how many of you have kept up with Secretary Hamilton's visit to North Korea. At first, it looked like after she travelled all the way, the top leadership in Pyongyang refused to see her, but look." He held up his screen as if the hundreds in the crowd could read the news headline. "*Secretary Hamilton Secures Meeting with North Korea's Top General,*" he read.

Hope swelled in Kennedy's chest, the same hope that just an hour earlier felt like it had died within her. As the crowd's cheers rose to a crescendo, Scott summarized the bullet points of the article. "They say it was confirmed that she was able to speak with the general about Ian's release, and she's scheduled to fly back to the States tomorrow."

CHAPTER 42

"That was some prayer service, wasn't it?" Scott held the car door open and helped Grandma Lucy into the backseat. "And I have to say it seems like pretty opportune timing with Secretary Hamilton just about to fly home from Pyongyang."

Grandma Lucy didn't respond. Kennedy turned around from the passenger seat to look at her. "I was really encouraged by your prayer," she said. "Thank you for that." She wondered if it was premature to make a connection between such a powerful prayer vigil and the Secretary of State's last day in Pyongyang.

Grandma Lucy smiled faintly, and Kennedy couldn't be quite sure if she'd heard or understood.

"Come on." Scott sat down on the driver side. "Let me take you two ladies to your hotel. It's been a long night, hasn't it, Grandma Lucy?"

Grandma Lucy didn't respond.

"Do you think she's all right?" Kennedy whispered. She hated talking about Grandma Lucy like that when she was right there, but she hadn't been acting like herself since she finished praying.

"My guess is she's just tired," Scott said. "Connie says it's hard for her to stay up late. I'll take you two straight to your room, then I've made plans to crash tonight with my buddy who lives out this way."

Kennedy was tired too, but that didn't stop her from worrying on the short drive to the hotel. Scott helped them check in, and with Grandma Lucy leaning on his arm, they all walked to the elevator.

"I think your prayers tonight made a huge difference," Scott told Grandma Lucy on the ride up, "not just for Ian but for the thousands of people living in North Korea."

She gave a faint nod, and the elevator doors opened.

Grandma Lucy had suffered a few heart attacks over the years. What if something happened while they were alone at the hotel? Kennedy pulled her cell phone out of her pocket, thankful and slightly surprised to find the battery fully charged. Well, at least if they needed anything, she'd have a way to call for help.

When Scott left, Kennedy asked Grandma Lucy if she needed any assistance getting ready for bed. Grandma Lucy shook her head. "I think I'll just lie down for a while if that's all right with you."

Kennedy felt silly pulling down the sheet and blankets, but Grandma Lucy didn't seem to mind. She reached out and took Kennedy's hand. "I believe the truth will set him free."

Kennedy leaned over and tucked Grandma Lucy in as if she were a little girl.

Ignoring the absurd urge to kiss the old woman good night, she patted her on the shoulder and simply whispered, "I sure hope you're right."

CHAPTER 43

Kennedy woke up early the next morning, still not having adjusted fully to Pacific time. She spent twenty minutes scanning news reports, and when Scott drove her to the airport, they listened to a talk-show host making speculations about the Secretary of State's visit to Pyongyang. Even though it was encouraging to hear Hamilton had finally managed to secure an audience with the North Korean general, nobody could confirm if she'd made any progress with Ian's case. There wouldn't be any more updates until the Secretary landed in DC later today.

More waiting.

"Thanks again for the ride and the good conversations and everything else," Kennedy said as Scott heaved her suitcase out of the trunk of his car.

"No prob. And hey, thanks for giving me an excuse to come out here and join your prayer vigil and hang out with my buddy last night. It was great."

"I'm glad to hear that." Kennedy opened the passenger side

door while airline announcements sounded in the background. "Bye, Grandma Lucy. I'm really glad we got to spend some time together." It was too hard to try to explain how encouraged Kennedy had felt after Grandma Lucy's prayer last night. She just hoped she could give her the smallest idea of how blessed she'd been. Even if the only reason Kennedy came to Seattle was to hear that one prayer, it was enough.

And even though nobody knew what Hamilton and the North Korean general had talked about in Pyongyang, there was always the chance the mission had been a success.

The chance Ian would be coming home.

How could Kennedy survive half a day on a plane not knowing anything?

Grandma Lucy smiled, looking much more rested than she had last night. Clasping Kennedy's hand in hers, she sang out in her rich voice, "May God bless you and keep you and make his glorious face to shine upon you. I don't know when we'll see each other again. I suppose it's here, there, or in the air, right?"

This time Kennedy did bend over to plant a small kiss on Grandma Lucy's wrinkled cheek. "Take care of yourself." She refused to think of what might happen to Ian if Grandma Lucy were to die while he was still imprisoned. Who would pray for him then?

"Have a safe flight home," Scott told her, leaving her and her suitcase on the airport curb.

***

It was the longest flight of her life. Kennedy turned on her cell phone as soon as her plane landed and jumped onto Channel 2's website. Secretary Hamilton should have arrived in DC by now. She had to find out what the Secretary had to say about her trip. Ian wasn't mentioned in any of the top headlines, but that could mean anything.

Her fingers shook while she typed his name into the search bar.

Hamilton returns Stateside without American reporter.

It would be all right, she told herself. As long as her lungs remembered how to breathe, it would be all right.

Inhale and exhale. Just like that.

So the Secretary's trip to Pyongyang wasn't the immediate success she'd hoped for. That was okay.

There would be other trips.

Diplomacy took time.

Time she wasn't sure Ian could spare.

All right, God. I have no idea what you're doing in this situation, but I'm going to trust that you have a plan for it all.

When she got off the plane, her breaths were even, her legs were steady, but her soul felt heavier than it ever had.

CHAPTER 44

"Kennedy!" Woong shouted in his shrill voice. "Kennedy!"

She stopped in the church hallway and turned around. "What's wrong?"

"I can't get this beard to stay on. I'm gonna be the only shepherd out there without any facial hair. It's an abomination!"

Kennedy tried to get the fake beard to stick with no success. "Your skin's just too soft."

He pouted, and then his eyes lit up. "Wait a minute. I got an idea." He reached into his pocket, pulled out a stick of gum, and shoved it into his mouth. Guessing his intentions and not necessarily wanting to find herself implicated in his plot, Kennedy walked downstairs, where Sandy had asked her to look for more candles.

They had to be down here someplace. Where did Sandy tell her to look?

"Kennedy?"

The voice startled her. "Oh, hi, Hannah. How's the baby?"

"She's perfect. She finally fell asleep, so I brought her down here where it's quiet."

"That's a good idea." The Christmas pageant would start in less than fifteen minutes, and the entire upper half of St. Margaret's church building was as chaotic as a Manhattan subway station, only with far more kids.

"I was sorry to hear the Secretary came back without your friend Ian," Hannah said.

"Thanks." Kennedy had been meaning to ask Hannah something about that and figured now might be as good a time as any. If only she could find those candles.

Oh, there they were.

"Kennedy!" Woong plodded down the stairs. "Mom wants to know if you found the candles yet and when you're gonna bring them up."

Kennedy passed the box to Woong and told him to hurry upstairs, then she pulled up a chair beside Hannah. "I know you want to keep it quiet for the baby, but can I ask you something?"

"Of course." Hannah had always been so calm and serene. Maybe that's why they had never spent much time together in Yanji even though they weren't far apart in age.

Kennedy stared at her hands, trying to figure out how to formulate the question she'd been mulling over since she returned to the East Coast.

"I know you don't talk much about what happened to you in North Korea, and I don't need to know any details," she hurried to add. "But I never actually heard the story of how you escaped."

She glanced at Hannah to make sure she hadn't asked anything inappropriate.

Hannah's face melted into a gentle smile. "Oh, it was Korea Freedom and their underground railroad. That's why I was so happy when your mom told me you were working for them last summer."

Kennedy shook her head. "That's not quite what I mean. I mean, before you got connected to Korea Freedom, before you even knew about the underground railroad. When you were still …" She hesitated to use the word. "When you were still in prison," she finally managed to get out.

Hannah nodded, but her smile had faded.

"It was the Lord," she answered. "We were all outside, there was a distraction, and I managed to get away."

"Was it dangerous?" What kind of stupid question was that? Of course it was dangerous.

Hannah nodded.

"But I mean, after ..." Why couldn't she think of the words she wanted to say? "When you got out, even after all the bad things that happened to you there, was it ... Did it make it hard for things to go back to normal after all that? After all you went through?"

She stared at Hannah's baby sleeping peacefully in her arms.

Hannah kept her voice low as if she were reciting nursery rhymes to her daughter. "Are you asking me if I was the same person after my time in prison?"

Kennedy nodded. Yes. That was exactly what she wanted to know.

Hannah sighed. "I wish I could give you a more hopeful response. And I know you're thinking about Ian and wondering what things will be like if he ever makes it home, but to be quite honest with you, the answer would be no." She shook her head and repeated the word. "No. I was never the same after that."

Kennedy let out her breath. That's what she had been afraid of.

CHAPTER 45

Nine days later

"Five. Four. Three. Two. One."

Kennedy forced herself to join the countdown while the small crowd in Carl and Sandy's living room watched the ball dropping on the television screen.

"Happy New Year!" everyone shouted, and Kennedy was hugged at least a dozen times, her ears ringing with the sound of the party horns Woong seemed particularly eager to use to welcome in the New Year.

Kennedy's mom handed her a glass of sparkling cider. "Drink up, honey. You know, New Year's a time for fresh starts." She lowered her voice. "And you know we all want you to be happy now, right?"

No, it was Kennedy who was trying to make her mom happy. That's why she suffered through a noisy pageant and an over-crowded Christmas Eve dinner and a plethora of presents at her parents' house and now this night of joy and festivities. The most important goal in Kennedy's life was to make it through the day without her mom sitting down and asking her if she needed to schedule extra counseling appointments or visit the doctor to see if her antidepressants needed to be adjusted.

It was for her mom that Kennedy smiled and drank the sparkling cider that stung her nose and clinked glasses with everyone in the Lindgrens' tiny house and put up with Woong throwing confetti all over her hair.

If Kennedy had her way, she would have locked herself in her bedroom and fallen asleep by nine. The last thing she needed was a reminder of how many months had passed with no word from Ian, no news about his case.

Kennedy's mom frowned at her. "Honey, are you sure you're all right? You don't look like you're having a very good time."

Her dad came up beside her. "Come on, Baby Cakes. Our Kensie girl's doing the best she can, isn't that right, kiddo?"

Her mom let out a melodramatic sigh. "Well, maybe we should tell her now. What do you think?"

Her dad lowered his voice. "I thought we were going to wait until tomorrow."

"I know, but she's miserable already. I don't see how it

could get much worse, honestly."

"Will you two please stop talking about me as if I weren't even here?" Kennedy didn't mind if her foul mood was ruining her parents' New Year's celebration. She couldn't stand the thought of one or both of them keeping secrets from her.

"What is it?" she demanded, staring at her parents both in turn.

It was her father who broke down first. "Princess, we got a letter from Connie, Ian's aunt back in Orchard Grove. It appears Ian managed to write one last letter ..."

"What do you mean last?" Her throat went dry.

"I knew we should have waited," her mom moaned.

"What do you mean last?" Kennedy demanded again, becoming aware by degrees that the guests around her had all stopped talking.

Her dad reached into his pocket. "This came in the mail two days ago. Connie warned us. Said maybe we should wait until after the holidays to let you ..."

"Give me that." Kennedy snatched the envelope out of his hands. "You mean you already opened it?"

"No, honey," her mom insisted. "That was just so we could read the note Connie wrote to us. We haven't seen the rest of it, but we do know what it ..." She stopped short when

Kennedy's dad cleared his throat.

"I'm sorry if you're mad at us, Kensie girl. Your mom and I thought it was best to wait, and Connie seemed to think so too." He shook his head. "It's not ... It's not the greatest of news."

Kennedy ignored his words. How had they received a letter and not given it to her right away? Who cared about what holiday the calendar claimed it was?

She turned her back to her parents and stared at the envelope. Sandy came up and wrapped her arm around her from the side. "You can go into the guest room if you'd like some time to yourself," she whispered.

Kennedy swallowed past the lump in her throat and nodded.

Her legs grew heavier with each step she took down the Lindgrens' hall. Her throat was parched even after a full glass of cider.

She walked into the guest room, turned on the light, and locked the door behind her.

Anything's better than not knowing, she told herself as she unfolded Ian's letter.

CHAPTER 46

Sweet, precious Kennedy, I'm so sorry to be writing you like this, and you'll have to forgive my atrocious handwriting too. I'm back at the hospital again. Doc doesn't think I'm going to make it. And that's not because he hasn't tried. I swear that man would give me one of his own lungs if he thought it could help.

I've got pneumonia. Funny, right? Strong, healthy man like me. I'm glad you can't see me like this. Wasting away wouldn't do it justice. And it's not just the pneumonia either. Doc says everything's shutting down one system at a time. There's nothing left to be done.

He's risking a lot letting me write you this one last letter, but I told him how important it was to me. He promised to find a way to slip it to the Swedish ambassador when he visits on Tuesday.

By then this letter may be all that's left of me.

There, how's that for melodrama?

I want you to know I've fought this disease. I've fought

as much as I can. And it's probably because of you that I'm still alive at this point. I keep remembering our summer together, all those long talks. How much I want to see you again. And that's what I'm fighting for.

The chance to tell you face to face how much I love you.

But you should see me now. No, scratch that. I'm glad you won't see me. This way you can remember me as I was then. Hehe, there's some more good melodrama for you.

I don't want you to be sad. I actually have good news for you. All those prayers Grandma Lucy's been praying for me (and I'm sure you have too) they've finally managed to work. It's a really long story, and I can't give you any details because if this letter gets intercepted I don't want to get anyone in trouble, but I understand now.

I've made my peace with God.

I'm ready to go home.

I have fought the good fight, right? Isn't that one of those Bible verses? I remember something about that at least.

I know someone literary like you is bound to pick up on the irony. You broke up with me because I wasn't a Christian. And now I am, but I'm on my deathbed (quite literally).

Maybe one day you can find it in your heart to share a little laugh with me.

I guess some things were only meant to be in heaven. But

don't worry. I don't expect you to die an old maid just so we can hook up when you join me there. I don't think it works like that. (I'm trying to be funny, by the way. Sorry if it comes across as morbid.)

We had a great time together, didn't we? And I'm not just talking about last summer. I still remember the day I saw you on the Red Line your first semester at Harvard. There was something in your eyes, something so sweet and innocent and trusting, something that reminded me that in spite of all the injustice I'd already seen around the world by that point, there were still things loving and beautiful. Things worth fighting for.

I love you, Kennedy. If it hadn't been for you, I probably would have died here and gone to an even more miserable fate, but now I know that I'm releasing my soul to Jesus, who has opened my eyes to show me how great a love he has even for a silly old blockhead like me.

I hope by now you and Grandma Lucy have grown close. It makes me happy to think of the two of you as friends.

And I thank God for the chance to tell you this one last goodbye.

I dream every night that I'm holding you in my arms, and for those short moments of bliss, I'm not cold or hungry or afraid.

You've done more for me than I could ever find words to thank you for even if I had the time (and the strength). Now go on and keep on doing great things for the kingdom of God. Maybe you don't see it, but he has used you already to advance his kingdom and fight against injustice and oppression in so many ways, and I'm so lucky to have known you and had you in my life.

All my love (and this time I'm not just being melodramatic),

Ian

CHAPTER 47

There was a knock on the door. "Kennedy? Kennedy?" It was her mother.

She opened her eyes enough to glance at the clock. Quarter after one.

"Kennedy?"

"Maybe we should just let her rest." She recognized her dad's muffled voice.

"What if she's hurt?"

"Here, I can unlock the door for you both."

Kennedy squeezed her eyes shut and held perfectly still while Sandy stepped in. She ran her hand across Kennedy's forehead and clucked her tongue. "Poor little lamb. She's fallen asleep."

"Should we wake her up?" her mom asked.

"What for?"

"That's right," Sandy agreed with her dad. "Why don't you two go on home whenever you're ready, and in the morning, I'll take her to your house or let you know when you can pick her up."

"I just hate the thought of her sad and all alone," her mom protested.

"She's asleep," her dad remarked. "The most merciful thing to do is let her rest."

The light turned off.

The door closed.

And Kennedy was once more completely alone.

PART THREE

CHAPTER 48

Mid February

Kennedy was glad this was her last semester. Even at a school like Harvard, professors were known to be lenient when grading the spring-semester seniors. She'd made her way through her last twelve credits in a mental haze that no amount of counseling sessions or anti-depressants could change. Finally, she told her therapist and her doctor and her parents that there was no reason for them to keep trying to make her happy. It wasn't like her brain was misfiring, telling her to act sad when life was perfectly fine.

She had every reason to mourn.

She refused to let anyone take that away from her.

It was mid-afternoon, and she trudged her way back toward her dorm where she would spend the evening munching on dry Cheerios, staring at her uncompleted syllabi and counting down the days to graduation. There was nothing more she could do for Ian. Even though the news outlets had never uncovered any more updates about his condition, she knew in her soul he was gone.

Now she had to find a way to say goodbye.

To move on.

She was even more determined to return to Seoul after graduation. By working with refugees at Korea Freedom's headquarters, she could honor Ian's memory.

It was the least she could do.

I love you, Kennedy. If it hadn't been for you, I may have died here and gone to an even more miserable fate, but now I know that I'm releasing my soul to Jesus, who has opened my eyes to show me how great a love he has even for a silly old blockhead like me.

She had memorized those lines from his parting letter. Actually, she had memorized the whole thing. Not an easy feat, seeing as how half of it was tear-stained after that awful New Year's Eve party.

Thankfully, her college classes gave her a reason to pretend to be busy. No more parents breathing down her neck like they had during Christmas break. Kennedy was having a hard enough time handling her own grief. She couldn't try to assuage her parents' guilt on top of her own.

She hadn't even tried to get in touch with Connie or Grandma Lucy. What would be the point? It was time to move on or at least try to. Things would be easier once the US embassy was able to confirm Ian's death. Maybe if they held a memorial service for him at Orchard Grove, she'd return one last time.

For now, it was simply a matter of existing through one day and into another. She'd grown so despondent she only returned about one out of every three or four of Willow's calls. Willow and Nick were even busier now, making plans to add on to their cabin to make room for all the extra foster kids they wanted to take in.

Everyone else was living their lives, but Kennedy was stuck in some timeless, emotionless existence. Yet another reason why she looked forward to graduation. Maybe Seoul would be the change in scenery she needed. And working with Korea Freedom, she wouldn't have as much time to sit around and mope, an art she'd perfected over the last few months.

She made her way into the dorm. It was only four, but she was thankful to be in for the night. No reason to run around campus when there was nowhere to go.

She walked toward her door and heard two familiar voices as she got closer to her room.

"Sandy? Carl? What are you doing here?"

Sandy jumped up from Kennedy's bed and dried her

eyes. "I'm sorry, dear. We didn't mean to startle you like this."

"How'd you get in my room?"

"Your RA let us in," she answered. "We explained we had some important news to share with you, and ..." Her face broke, and she buried herself behind a tissue.

Kennedy glanced to Carl. What was going on?

Sandy blew her nose loudly. "Have you eaten anything, dear? Are you hungry?"

What kind of question was that?

Sandy cleared her throat. "We got a call from Ian's aunt Connie. She said she's been trying to get hold of you and couldn't."

Kennedy didn't answer.

Sandy wiped her face again. "It's the kind of news we wanted to tell you in person, honey. We want you to know we'll always be here for you, Carl and me both ..."

"Oh, will you spit it out, woman?" Carl interrupted. "I know you said that you wanted to be the one to tell her, and I went along with it, but look at the poor girl's face. It's like you're about to tell her the family dog's been run over by the dump truck."

"Poor Snoopy," Sandy murmured.

"Huh?"

"Will you just tell her?" Carl bellowed.

"Okay, you're absolutely right." Sandy reached out for her husband's hand. "What Carl and I came over here to say, it's about Ian. I think I told you that already, and his aunt wanted you to hear before it made the evening news …"

"Oh, let me do it." Carl put both hands on Kennedy's shoulders. "Congratulations, Kennedy. Your boyfriend's alive, and Secretary Hamilton is flying him home as we speak."

CHAPTER 49

Kennedy had never been more thankful to be tired and jetlagged. She hadn't bothered to carry anything besides what would fit in her backpack so she could take a cab directly from the airport to the hospital in Seattle where Ian was being treated.

The details of his release were still coming in, but Kennedy didn't care who had gotten him home or how. All she wanted was assurance that he really was alive and that he was going to survive.

Connie had told her by phone, and her parents had both issued dire warnings as well, that she needed to be prepared for the worst. When she saw him, he was going to look awful (*think Holocaust survivor,* her dad had said, planting a very helpful image in her mind), and his recovery would probably have to be measured in months and not weeks or days.

It didn't matter.

He was here.

Nothing else was important, not even her schoolwork,

which is why she had insisted her parents get her just a one-way ticket. They were reluctant until she got emails from two out of her three professors stating she could turn in her assignments by email so she wouldn't fall too behind. Her only other class just had one more final paper and test, and even if Kennedy failed, she had taken enough credits early on in her college career she could still graduate in May.

She had memorized his room number and already looked up directions by the time she arrived at the hospital. She sprinted nearly the whole way and ended up taking three flights of stairs instead of standing around waiting for an elevator.

She was going to see Ian.

Hurrying past nurses in scrubs and orderlies with their clipboards, she scanned the room numbers, which turned out to be an unnecessary practice. Of course his room would be the one guarded by Feds.

Funny. Just like in the movies. Two men in black suits, walkie talkies, the works. She'd have to tell Ian he'd turned into a walking cliché.

"I'm Kennedy Stern," she told the first official. "Ian's expecting me."

He shook his head. "No visitors."

"I've been talking with his aunt. She knows I'm

coming."

"No visitors," he repeated.

"Oh, Kennedy!" Connie called out from down the hallway.

Kennedy hurried toward her. "Is he okay?" she asked. "The men said I couldn't go in ..."

Connie frowned. "I'm sorry, sweetie. It turns out, well ..." She bit her lip and looked over one of Kennedy's shoulders and then the other before lowering her voice. "He's in a mood today. Doctor says it's totally normal, but he, um ..." She cleared her throat. "He doesn't want to see anyone."

What?

"I just flew in," Kennedy argued, as if that should change everyone's mind. "I ... Is he all right?"

Connie frowned. "He's self-conscious, sweetie. I'm sure that's it. He's lost a lot of weight, and, well ... Here. You let me go in and talk some sense into that boy. No nephew of mine is going to turn away his girlfriend who's come all this way just to see him, no matter how he looks. You just wait here, and I hate to say it, but you better start preparing yourself."

As if Kennedy hadn't spent the past nine hours of travel doing exactly that.

Connie bustled past the two guards and slipped into the

room. A minute later, she nudged the door open and beckoned Kennedy over.

"Come on. He's asleep. Let her in," she told the officers in an authoritative voice. "This is his girlfriend."

It wasn't until she stepped into the room that Kennedy finally understood what Connie and her parents and everyone else had been trying to warn her about. He looked like a corpse. Not Ian, not the man she loved and had grieved over. His hair was thin and hung in clumps against his pale face. The sunken cheekbones were hard enough to take in, but even with his hospital robe on, Kennedy could see his ribs sticking out. Watched the way his collarbone pulled with each breath he took.

"Come on." Connie took her hand and led her to the bedside.

It was confirmed.

She hated hospitals.

Tears stung her eyes. She had to look away.

"It's all right," Connie assured her. "In fact, he's looking stronger than he did when they first brought him in."

Kennedy couldn't imagine anyone looking closer to death. She shook her head. "Maybe I should have waited to come."

"No," Connie argued. "He wants to see you. Really he does. He just doesn't know it yet."

Small comfort, seeing as how Kennedy had rushed all the way over from Boston just to be with him.

Connie's phone beeped. "Oh, that's Grandma Lucy. You wait here. I'll just be a minute." Without giving Kennedy the chance to protest, Connie slipped out of the room, leaving Kennedy alone with this ghost of the man she had once known and loved.

CHAPTER 50

Yes, she had definitely made a mistake coming to Seattle.

What did she expect? For Ian to be sitting in his hospital bed, smiling at her and ready to play a few rounds of Scrabble?

Tears streaked down her cheeks. Hot and angry tears.

Why, God? You brought him home, but like this?

Maybe she was no better than the Israelites in the desert, grumbling for meat when God had so recently fed them manna, but she didn't care.

She didn't want to leave him alone, but she didn't want to stay. How long was Connie going to take?

"You sure you want to go now, Kensie girl?" her dad had asked. "It might make more sense to let him recover some of his strength first."

He'd tried to warn her, and she had ignored him. Like some silly girl with a Florence Nightingale complex, she had it in her head that being here would bring Ian the peace and healing he needed.

Stupid, stupid, stupid.

Shouldn't she have learned by now that her dad was always right?

Good thing she'd bought a one-way ticket. That way she could go home immediately. Back to Cambridge, back to her cold, lonely dorm, back to her Cheerios and Craisins ...

"Kennedy?"

Oh, no. He was awake. What was she supposed to do? He wasn't supposed to see her here.

Why had she come?"

"Kennedy?"

"I'm sorry. I was just leaving." She turned so he couldn't see her tears, even though her voice made it obvious she was crying.

His next few words were garbled. "... missed you so much."

She couldn't do this. Every word he spoke was raspy, the rattling in his lungs so pronounced she felt vicariously lightheaded.

"I'm going to see where Connie is." She still couldn't bring herself to turn around. What had she done? Injuries like his, illnesses like his, trauma like his needed time to heal. She was never meant to see him this way. No wonder he told the guards not to let in any visitors.

"... don't want you to leave."

"I can't ..." she started to stammer and then stopped. Beneath the rattling lungs, beneath the unbearable wheezing, she heard something she recognized.

She forced her body to turn around, demanded herself to stop crying.

Their eyes met.

"You came."

At first, she was afraid he'd be mad to see her here, but the look in his eyes, hollow as they were, wasn't anger.

She stepped forward. "I came. I needed to see you. I thought you ..." She stopped herself when the tears started leaking down once more. "I thought you were gone."

Why had he done this to her? Why had he written her that letter from the hospital? Why had he forced her to go through these months of mourning all alone?

Emotionally, she was as much of a ghost as he was.

How could he have been so cruel?

"Don't be sad." His face was so emaciated it reminded her of the grimace on a Halloween skull. "Please don't be sad." His chest heaved. Was this how skeletons cried?

He reached out his hand, bony with red and black lesions on the skin. Bruises. What had happened to him?

"I missed you," he repeated. "So much."

She took his hand, surprised that it felt warm. She'd been prepared for the tepid temperature of a cadaver.

"I missed you too." She bathed the sores on his hand with her tears. "I stopped praying for you. I'm so sorry. I thought you were dead."

"Shh." He was the one comforting her now. "Shh," he repeated. "That's all over. It's all in the past. We're together now. Nothing else matters."

For a fleeting moment, Kennedy forgot about his raspy breath, about whatever physical and emotional wounds he bore and how long it would take for him to heal.

She forgot about the assignments she'd have to complete if she wanted to graduate in May. She forgot about her obligations back in Cambridge, forgot about how eager she'd so recently been to run back to her dorm.

For a fleeting moment, all those details disappeared.

Ian was alive.

He would survive.

God would heal each and every one of his wounds, both those she could see and those she couldn't.

And she would be there to pray for him and encourage him while he regained his strength, no matter what it cost her.

In that moment, she knew she loved him and he loved her.

In that moment, nothing else mattered.

CHAPTER 51

February 18 — "That's great!"

Even though Ian had asked her not to make a big deal about it, Kennedy couldn't contain her excitement. "You're doing great," she squealed. "Keep it up."

He landed back in bed after walking three laps with his nurse around the room and collapsed, breathless, on his pillow.

"You really enjoy watching me suffer, don't you?" he asked.

"Just keep getting stronger," she said, and he promised he would try.

February 22 — "I swear if I have to eat one more hospital meal, I'm going throw my mashed potatoes against the wall, just like a VeggieTale."

"So I guess it's a good sign you're getting sassy."

"I'm not sassy. I'm hungry."

"Well, that's a good sign too. You're getting your appetite back."

He grinned at her. "Yeah, easy for you to say since you can walk yourself down to that cafeteria any time you want. And what about me? I'm wasting away here!" He laughed, still excited about the four pounds he'd gained since he arrived in Seattle.

February 24 — "Hey, no fair. You promised me you wouldn't cry."

Kennedy sniffed and tried to look cheerful. "I'm sorry. It's just going to be so hard not to see you every day."

He pulled her face close toward him and pressed her forehead against his. "Look at it this way. If you don't go back to campus now, you're not going to graduate. If you don't graduate, you're not going to med school. And if you don't make it to med school, how are you going to nurse me back to health?"

She laughed. "I certainly hope you don't expect me to wait on you like this once they discharge you from the hospital."

He stroked her hair, his eyes gleaming. "Of course I do. Why do you think I allowed myself to get so sick in the first place?"

Their smiles faded. The laughter ceased.

He cleared his throat and lowered his voice. "Go back to

campus now. I'll be fine. You heard the doctor say so himself. And to be quite honest, I think you being here so much has made Connie jealous. Seriously, you'll be doing her a favor. Once you're gone, she can do nothing but take care of me all day long."

"You're so spoiled," Kennedy teased even though her heart was heavy.

"One more kiss before you go?" he asked.

"Of course."

March 3 — "Hey, you ready for our big date?"

She smiled. "Some date with you lying in bed three thousand miles away."

"Oh, great," he joked. "Way to spoil the romance. Come on. What movie are we watching tonight?"

"Well, I figured I'd give you two choices." She did her best to match his playful tone. "We could do *Mr. Smith Goes to Washington*, or if you're feeling particularly adventurous, we can watch *To Kill a Mockingbird*."

The video image of his smile on her laptop warmed her almost as much as if they'd been in the same room together.

"I could use me a good old-fashioned filibuster."

She pressed a few buttons on her computer. "Mr. Smith it is."

March 14 — "How's your appetite? Are you still gaining weight?"

"Sheesh," he whined. "You're as bad as my aunt. I swear if I don't eat three helpings of everything she's made she'll sit and literally start to cry, just like a little baby."

"Oh, she's probably just crying tears of joy that she doesn't have to hire someone else to take care of all her beloved goats while she nurses you in Seattle anymore. Are you managing the stairs to the attic okay?"

"Hey, I'm a recovering pneumonia patient with a flaming case of PTSD that gives me terrible flashbacks, but that doesn't make me a gimp."

"Really?" she teased. "Because the last time I was out there, you needed an entire cheerleading section just to make it to the toilet and back."

"Well, I always did think you'd look good in one of those short little cheerleading skirts."

"Stop it or your aunt will hear."

"Oh, she's listening right now. Say hi to Connie."

"What? Are you serious?"

His laugh rang out and echoed in her dorm room. "No, I'm joking. Now, are we going to do that Bible study or what? Or do I need to wait until next week when you come visit? Because I was planning for things to be real serious then too, but I'm not necessarily talking about the studying."

March 17 — "This has been the longest semester of my life." She leaned her head against his chest, and he ran his fingers through her hair.

"You two want some popcorn?" Connie poked her head into the living room.

"We're fine," he answered somewhat tersely.

"Well, don't forget that Kennedy's been in the air all day. Poor thing's probably starving."

"Trust me," he said, "I know what starving is, and she's not even close. Actually, wait, I better check to make sure." He tickled her ribs. "Nope. Not starving yet. But I'll let you know if that changes."

March 19 — He was laughing so hard he doubled over. "I'll never forget your face when you saw that goat just pop out. For a minute, I thought I was going to have to drop the kid and come catch you before you fainted."

"It wasn't that bad," she insisted while the newborn goat tried to suckle her finger.

"How in the world are you going to be a doctor if you get woozy at the sight of blood? Oh, never mind. You can do anything you set your mind to. I know that much about you at least."

"I wasn't woozy," she insisted. "You just didn't tell me there'd be so much blood."

"This is childbirth," he replied. "What'd you expect?"

"Something a little more sterile and a lot less messy," she answered honestly.

March 23 — It was so nice to feel the strength in his arms when he hugged her goodbye.

"I'm going to miss you," he said, speaking into the top of her head.

"I'm going to miss you too."

"Just another month, though. Then finals, and then bam. You'll be a college graduate, and we'll all be there together celebrating your bachelor's. Have I told you lately that I'm proud of you?"

"Yeah, I think I've heard that once or twice before."

He kissed her forehead. "It's true. You are the most amazing woman I've ever met. You know that, don't you?"

"More amazing than a certain Miss Abby?" she teased.

He shook his head. "I still can't believe Connie told you that whole story. But you're joking, right? You're not seriously jealous or anything are you?"

She wrapped her arms around him. "Why would I be jealous when I have you all to myself?"

He nuzzled his nose against hers. "Don't you forget it. Now go catch that plane, study hard, and I'll see you at graduation, all right?"

"All right."

She picked up her suitcase and turned to go.

"Oh, and Kennedy?"

"Yeah?"

"I love you. Have I told you that?"

"I've heard that once or twice before."

CHAPTER 52

Graduation Day

"I've just got to hug you one more time." Sandy reached over and swallowed Kennedy in her embrace.

"Thanks." She glanced at the Lindgrens' clock. What was taking Ian and his grandma so long? Had they gotten lost on the way to the house?

"You looked darling in that cap and gown," Sandy said. "Feels like just yesterday you were in Cambridge on your own for the very first time. And now look at you, a real college graduate with a diploma and everything."

Kennedy didn't have the heart to tell her that the piece of paper the dean handed to her on the stage was just for show. The real thing would be mailed out to her parents' address sometime over the summer.

She glanced again at the clock.

"Where is that boy of yours?" Sandy asked.

"He'll be here soon." Carl came out from the bedroom,

where he'd changed out of his collared shirt and tie, and wrapped Kennedy up in a hug just as big as his wife's had been. "We are so happy and honored that we get to share this special day with you."

"Thanks." Besides her parents, who were out picking up the cake, and Ian, who was on his way over with Grandma Lucy, Kennedy couldn't think of anyone else she'd be happier to share today with.

Woong ran out from his bedroom holding a Lego spaceship. "Pew! Pew! Pew!" he shouted. "Destroy the evil scientist!" He aimed the guns at Kennedy.

"Watch where you're pointing that thing, son," Sandy chided.

The doorbell rang. Sandy grinned at her. "That's probably your man. Go on. Open it. You look stunning, by the way, an absolute jewel."

Kennedy threw open the door. Ian and Grandma Lucy had flown in late last night. Other than a quick chat while she and her dad drove them from the airport to their hotel, she'd hardly had the chance to see him.

He squeezed her tight and lifted her off the floor. "Not bad for a man who was halfway starved just a few months ago, right?"

Kennedy giggled. When he set her down, Grandma Lucy

took her hands in hers. "I am so very blessed to be here. So very blessed. I couldn't think of a more beautiful day to celebrate all your accomplishments or a more wondrous God who's brought us all together again."

CHAPTER 53

The sun had set, and Woong was in bed by the time Sandy filled all the glasses with sparkling cider. It was almost ten, but Kennedy's whole body was reacting to the excitement of the day. She could probably go a full week without sleep.

Her dad cleared his throat and raised his glass. "To my daughter Kennedy. I know you probably hate hearing this story, but I'll never forget the day your mother and I brought you home to our tiny little apartment during the biggest blizzard on record. You were such a tiny little thing, and when I stopped at a red light, I started crying. Your mom thought it was because I was scared of being a dad, but I was overwhelmed by how beautiful and perfect you were, and I can't begin to express the way God completed my life the day you were born.

"Kensie girl, I've watched you change and grow from wanting nothing more than to become a horse trainer, to a bomb squad technician, to the first woman to travel to Mars.

And I've watched the way you've handled yourself through every difficult situation God has brought your way, and believe me, it wasn't easy, especially with your mother and me on the other side of the world, only able to watch and pray."

He let out a sound that was a half laugh, half cough. "You probably won't understand this until you have kids of your own one day, but your mother and I have prayed for you so much, and today it feels like every single one of those blessings we've asked God to grant you has been fulfilled. You're a college graduate. You have a wonderful year ahead of you in Seoul before you go on to finish your training as a doctor. And as if that weren't enough, you have a strong, godly boyfriend ..."

Her mother nudged him in the side. Kennedy laughed and held up her left hand while her dad cleared his throat. "Excuse me. You have a strong, godly *fiancé* as of" — he checked his wrist — "about twenty minutes ago, and I couldn't be happier for you or prouder of the woman you are, the woman God is creating you to be."

He leaned over and gave her a hug. "Now, you and Ian probably haven't had time to formulate all your plans, but Ian, I hope you know how grateful my wife and I are to have you in Kennedy's life, and when you're not traveling the world doing your documentaries or spending time in Seoul with my daughter planning your wedding, I hope you know our home is always open to you. I've never had a son, and I have no idea what it's like to be a father-in-law either, but I'm excited for this chance to learn."

He raised his glass. "To Kennedy, with congratulations for graduating *summa cum laude*, with prayers for a safe trip to Seoul and a wonderful year serving the Lord with Korea Freedom International. And to the happy couple, may God bless you, lead you, and bring you both all the encouragement and love and wisdom you need to please him in all you do."

The guests raised their glasses and murmured their agreement.

Kennedy looked up to kiss her fiancé, and out of the corner of her eye, she saw Grandma Lucy standing in the background, arms outstretched, eyes raised toward heaven, lips forming silent prayers that seemed to surround the entire gathering before floating up to heaven, where she was certain they found their audience in the throne room of God.

A NOTE FROM THE AUTHOR

In 2013, I published a novel about Christian persecution in North Korea. At the time, I didn't imagine *The Beloved Daughter* turning into a suspense series set in North Korea. Nor did I anticipate that some of those novels would feature an American missionary couple, Roger and Juliette Stern, whose daughter had just left home for her first semester at Harvard University.

In 2015, Kennedy got a book of her own. My thought was to give myself and my readers a break from the heavy themes in the Whispers of Refuge series and offer something more accessible. In short, I had planned for the Kennedy books to be some "light Christian reading," which if you've followed the series at all probably has you chuckling as much as it does me.

Captivated is the last book in the Kennedy Stern series. I wish I had the eloquence to more adequately express how grateful I am for the kind words and encouragement I have received from my readers. You truly have given momentum to this series. It wouldn't exist if it weren't for you.

The Kennedy Stern series is complete, but there are many characters introduced in this last novel that appear in other books you might enjoy. Grandma Lucy, Connie, and the goats of Safe Anchorage Farm are characters in two different Washington-based series. The Sweet Dream novels are romances set in Orchard Grove. You can start with book one, *What Dreams May Come*, the story of the missionary Scott you met in *Captivated*.

This small town in apple country, Washington, is also the setting for the Orchard Grove Women's Fiction series featuring true-to-life couples struggling with real-to-life issues that bring them face-to-face with the one true God.

And if you haven't read them yet, the *Whispers of Refuge* novels are the North Korean books where you'll more thoroughly meet Kennedy's parents (*Slave Again*), Hannah (*Torn Asunder*), and Woong (*Flower Swallow*). So just because we're saying goodbye (for now) to Kennedy Stern, this certainly isn't the end, as I hope and pray for God to provide me with many more stories to share with you over the years. If you'd like to read the novel about Ian's captivity in North Korea, buy *Out of North Korea* today.

www.ingramcontent.com/pod-product-compliance
Ingram Content Group UK Ltd.
Pitfield, Milton Keynes, MK11 3LW, UK
UKHW041348210225
4701UKWH00033B/264